- Please return items before closing time
  on the last date stamped to avoid charges.
- Renew books by phoning 01305 224311 or
  online www.dorsetforyou.com/libraries
- Items may be returned to any Dorset library.
- Please note that children's books issued on
  an adult card will incur overdue charges.

Dorset County Council
Library Service

DL/2372 dd05450

The Ghosts of
Neddingfield Hall

The Ghosts of Neddingfield Hall

Fenella-Jane Miller

.LE · LONDON

ISBN 978-0-7090-8690-1

Robert Hale Limited
Clerkenwell House
Clerkenwell Green
London EC1R 0HT

www.halebooks.com

Typeset in 11/15½pt Palatino
Printed and bound in Great Britain by
MPG Biddles Limited, King's Lynn

Dedication

Again for my wonderful, irreplaceable children
Annabel and Lincoln

Prologue

June 1814

LORD COLEBROOK, THE Earl of Waverly admired himself in his new finery. The coat he'd had made at Weston's in royal blue superfine had shoulders padded to give him extra width and his new boots, from Hoby, had lifts in the heel making him two inches taller.

His hair, cut in a fashionable Brutus style, would have been better hidden under an old-fashioned powdered wig, as it was quite definitely thinning on top and its rich russet tones were fading to an indeterminate sandy colour. He smiled, his thin lips and aquiline nose, he felt, added to his elegance and, dressed as he now, he was obviously a member of the aristocracy.

He could hardly believe that the young lawyer he had employed to find out as much about his English relatives as he could, had come up with the information that he had inherited a title, and along with it three sizeable properties and a fortune in the funds.

Lord Colebrook had employed him to ferret out facts about Neddingfield Hall and Miss Culley who was, in his opinion, living there illegally. His grandfather had grown up at Neddingfield, but, as the youngest son, had had no expectations of inheriting. He and his two brothers had spent their summers rampaging around the Kent countryside, and it was his grand-father, after whom he was named, who had rediscovered the underground cellar in which visiting priests had been secreted after they'd landed from the Continent in the reign of Queen Elizabeth.

It was a short step from there to becoming involved with the local free-traders, and he had the ideal place for them to hide their contraband when it first arrived on the coast. The young man had become rich from his ill-gotten gains, but, unfortu-nately, the excise men had captured him one night on the beach. His hideout had remained undiscovered, but he was given the option of going to live on the far side of the world, out of sight of the family, or being hanged as a common felon.

Thus Bertram had been born in the Caribbean; he'd never met his grandfather, but his father had filled his head with tales of Neddingfield Hall, and how it should belong to them, should never have been passed down the female line. He was a Sinclair; the current owner was a Culley.

He heard the rattle of teacups approaching; the refreshments he had requested were on their way. He relaxed his expression to one of supreme indifference, and turned to face the door. There was a polite tap and he bade the servant enter.

'I have your tray, my lord; shall I put it on the side table?'

'Do that. I'm expecting Mr Jones, my lawyer, to arrive later this afternoon. Show him in immediately.' The footman bowed and left him on his own again.

He loved to hear himself addressed as '*my lord*', in fact he sent for unwanted items just so he could hear his servants address him so. He had grown up in near poverty, until his father had become involved in the trade of black gold. In this way he had restored their fortunes, and when he had died in the New Year, he'd made Bertram promise to return to England and reclaim his rightful heritage.

His money had been transferred to London. An agent had purchased him this smart townhouse, not in the most fashionable part of London, but at the time he had no expectations of being elevated to the peerage. He'd brought with him three faithful retainers, those with as little compunction for fair dealing as he had; who were not squeamish in the slightest and would, indeed had, dispatch anyone who stood in his way without hesitation.

The lawyer he had selected carefully was recently qualified, with little more than one room and a clerk to assist him. He had no wish for his business to become bandied about the coffee houses. The man, Jones, had respectable lodgings, but no wife or dependants which made him ideal. He had been gathering information about Miss Culley, the current state of Neddingfield Hall, and her heir, a Major Sinclair, currently fighting in France.

His eyes gleamed with satisfaction. With luck the major would meet his end there, leaving him the sole legitimate heir and then he would have no need to become embroiled in an unsavoury Machiavellian plot in order to obtain what he wanted.

His intention was to be the owner of Neddingfield Hall before the end of the year. He knew he no longer needed it, but he had promised his father on his deathbed that his remote branch of the family would be reinstalled there and so had no intention of reneging on his promise.

He sat down to study the papers he had already received. Miss Culley had inherited the property from her mother, who had been a Sinclair until her marriage. The house was not entailed, or it would have gone directly to this major. As far as he knew there were no other relatives in his way.

The mantel clock struck three and he heard footsteps approaching the drawing-room. Jones, as usual, was punctual. Once again he posed, leaning nonchalantly against the mantelshelf, his legs crossed at the ankle, the epitome of elegance, or so he thought.

Mr Jones entered. For some reason the man's face was pale, his hands trembling. This was not his normal demeanour and, for a horrible moment, Bertram thought the man had contracted a putrid fever and brought it into his house.

'Are you unwell, sir? Pray, do not come any closer; I have no wish to catch whatever it is you're suffering from.' He spoke from the relative safety of the window embrasure, the long curtains on either side almost obscuring him from view.

'No, sir, I am not unwell, but am the bearer of the most awful tidings. I hardly know how to tell you.'

Bertram stepped forward, his face a mask of anger. How dare this man address him so informally? He was about to reprimand him sharply when his brain registered that the omission had been deliberate.

He grasped the back of a chair, his knuckles white. 'What is it you have to tell me? Do not procrastinate, Jones, I wish to know the whole, leave out no details.'

Slowly the man stumbled out the shocking news. 'I was misinformed, Mr Sinclair, the title is to be given to a Ralph Sinclair, whose claim is thought to be a degree closer. However no one can find him. He's somewhere on the Continent with the Duke of Wellington and until he can be contacted is unaware of his elevation.'

To be so cruelly demoted by a man he already hated was too much for his slender grip on sanity. 'Excuse me, Mr Jones, I have forgotten a most urgent errand.'

His lawyer, his colour better now he believed his employer had accepted his news with equanimity, nodded politely. 'I'm perfectly content here, sir; I am in no hurry to return to my lodgings, my time is yours.'

Bertram strode from the room and took the back stairs that led to a small cubby hole in which his three henchman remained when not occupied about his business. It took him moments to explain what he required and then he was back in his drawing-room, the perfect urbane gentleman. When he dismissed his lawyer it was with a friendly smile. The butler who conducted him to the front door remarked on the young man's improved appearance.

Mr Jones was never seen again. When his landlady eventually reported his non-appearance he had already been dead for a week. His clerk, strangely, had also disappeared, the office denuded of papers. The constabulary believed the man had taken advantage of his employer's absence and absconded with his documents.

Bertram Sinclair, satisfied no one would ever know he had coveted the title, or that he had made extensive enquiries about Neddingfield Hall, spent the next few weeks devising an ingenious plot that would reinstate him as Lord Colebrook and also give him what he desired most: Neddingfield Hall. He would make his preparations carefully; he had no need to hurry, revenge was a dish best eaten cold.

Chapter One

November 1815

'GOOD HEAVENS! I wonder why we've stopped this time? Birdie, is it that wretched coach we have been forced to travel behind this past two hours, holding us up?'

The grey-haired lady Miss Hester Frobisher was addressing so informally, shook her head in frustration. 'My dear girl, how can I possibly know why we've stopped? If you want to find out, why don't you open the window and hang out like an urchin? I'm sure the aristocrat travelling ahead of us would find the spectacle amusing.'

Hester giggled. 'You're quite right, as usual, Birdie. I suppose I must remain here on the seat, and pretend that I am a meek and docile young woman, content to do as I'm bid.'

The snort of derision from her companion woke what at first glance might have been taken for an old black rug crumpled up on the opposite squab. 'Oh dear, now Jet has woken up. I shall have to get out and let him—'

'Thank you, my dear girl, I'm well aware what that smelly animal will wish to do. What possessed you to bring him with us, I cannot imagine. All I can say it's a consolation, albeit a small one, that we are travelling in November and not at the height of summer. Being incarcerated with your malodorous dog would have been unbearable in the heat.'

Hester leant over, impulsively kissing the leathery cheek of her dearest friend and companion, Miss Mary Bird. 'Hush, Birdie, you'll offend him. You know how clever he is, he understands every word you say.'

Kicking aside the bricks placed in the well of the carriage to keep their feet warm that morning, Hester tightened the ties of her bonnet and pulled her cloak firmly about her shoulders. The black hearthrug stood up arching his back, emitting a stream of noxious gas as he did so. At the sound of her companion choking she hastily flung open the carriage door and, without waiting for the steps to be let down, jumped out on to the lane, closely followed by her dog.

A swirl of icy wind tugged at her cloak and her bonnet threatened to leave her head in spite of the tightness of its ribbons. She glanced down the lane, seeing at once what was causing the hold-up. The smart equipage, its navy-blue coachwork gleaming in the late afternoon sunlight, was stationary a hundred yards ahead of them.

Then Hester noticed that the gates of her great-aunt Agatha's ancestral home, Neddingfield Hall, were closed across the driveway. Even from this distance she could see they had been barred from the inside.

She turned, clutching her bonnet with one hand and the neck of her cloak with the other, to speak to one of the two outriders who had accompanied her on this trip. Tom, more her man of affairs than a common servant, was astride her own gelding, Thunder, a magnificent bay.

'Tom, why have we stopped so far away? I should really have liked to have gained sight of the other travellers.'

The young man called down to her, his words almost blown away by the wind. 'If we got any closer, miss, Bill won't be able to turn the coach. It's going to be a tight squeeze as it is. It's a rum do, the gates being closed, I don't remember them being like this before.'

'No, they never have. It's very worrying. Why should Aunt Agatha summon me urgently and then bar the road?'

As she was talking, the watery sun slowly sank below the horizon and the road took on a gloomy, almost threatening atmosphere. 'Jet's in the bushes; I shall wait with him whilst Bill turns the carriage. We cannot stand about out here, we shall have to put up at the Jug and Bottle and discover what has happened tomorrow.'

Hurrying across the lane, she followed the sound of her dog crashing about in the undergrowth. She prayed he wouldn't pick up the scent of a rabbit and refuse to return to her call. She loved him dearly, but sometimes she did wish he was a little more obedient.

Hester could hear Tom and James assisting Bill to turn the horses. It was fortuitous they were tired, as the four matching chestnuts would never have submitted to such cavalier treatment when they'd set off that morning.

She wondered who the occupants of the other travelling carriage were; that they were members of the aristocracy was perfectly clear from the gilt-encrusted crest emblazoned on the side of the coach. She hadn't been aware that her aunt mixed with the *ton*; she was an eccentric, had never married. She lived as she pleased on the vast fortune left her by doting parents. The money had been made in shipping, and Hester knew she stood to gain an absolute fortune when Aunt Agatha died. However, as Miss Culley was a healthy woman in her sixties this was immaterial.

There was a second noise in the woodland ahead. In the dark she couldn't make out what it was, but she felt hairs on the back of her neck stand up. Instinctively she called her dog. She heard him crashing back and the sound of his rumbling growl did nothing to reassure her. Instead of pausing at her side, the dog shot past, hackles up, looking more like a wolf than a domestic animal. Suddenly she was no longer alone.

'What ails that dog, Miss Frobisher?' Tom was beside her, his pistol out, staring into the darkness.

'I don't know, I thought I heard someone out there. Jet obviously thinks there's a danger.'

'In that case, miss, come back to the coach. There's something havey-cavey about all this: locked gates, a stranger in front of us. I think the sooner we get back to Little Neddingfield the better.'

Hester found herself bundled back through the undergrowth and out on to the lane. 'I'm not leaving without Jet.' She didn't have to wait long, minutes later her hound appeared at her side, his neck smooth, his tongue lolling and eyes shining with pleasure. 'Good dog, come along, we've got to go.'

Scrambling back inside, her dog followed, flopping down on the far seat as if by right. James slammed the door and the coach lurched off, leaving whoever it was in the other vehicle to follow, or not, as they pleased.

'Birdie, what about Jet? The last time I had occasion to visit the Jug and Bottle I was struck by its cleanliness. I rather think that Mrs Jarvis will not welcome his presence in our bedchamber.'

'And neither shall I, my dear. The dog can sleep outside in the stables with Thunder; you know he's just as happy there, as he is cooped up inside with you.'

Hester sighed; this was quite true. She believed one's faithful hound should pine away without one's presence, but Jet indeed seemed to thrive in her absence. No, that wasn't quite true, he was only happy if he knew she was within easy reach.

The coach turned sharply right and halted. 'Well, my dear, here we are. I must own I'm a mite uncomfortable after being in here all day. I wish to stretch my legs and wash the grime from my person.'

Before Hester could reply, the door swung open and Tom let down the steps. 'I have managed to obtain two chambers and a private parlour for you, Miss Frobisher.' He grinned and Hester thought she detected a malicious glint in his eye. 'The only rooms left are of a poor quality.'

She hid a smile behind her gloved hand. When the smart coach arrived, its occupants would have nowhere suitable to sleep. It didn't bother her one jot.

'Come along, Birdie. If I remember correctly Mrs Jarvis sets an excellent table so we shall not go hungry tonight.' She noticed James had slipped a loop of rope around Jet's neck and was holding him firmly. She saw the dog look up, assessing his captor, and then relax. Satisfied, she hurried in to the warmth of the inn, glad to get out of the biting wind.

A jolly, middle-aged lady in a pristine apron came forward to greet her. 'Good evening, Miss Frobisher, Miss Bird. I'm so pleased to be able to help you out tonight. What a to-do! Your man explained that you're unable to reach Neddingfield Hall. No doubt everything will be explained right enough tomorrow. I'll show you to your chambers myself, if you would care to come this way.'

The landlady, remarkably nimble for one of her size, lifted her skirts and swept across the polished boards to the oak staircase. She glanced over her shoulder encouragingly. 'Your parlour overlooks the yard; you'll be able to see all the comings and goings. However, your bedchamber, Miss Frobisher, is at the back of the building so you won't be disturbed.'

Hester gathered up the folds of her voluminous cloak and ran up behind Mrs Jarvis. She was so fatigued she didn't think an army marching past could rouse her that night.

Ten minutes later she was in her room removing her gown and preparing to wash in the bowl of hot water that had arrived almost as she did. She had dispensed with the luxury of her own maid for this short trip; so Jane had been left behind. Hester thought she was quite capable of doing for herself for a short space of time. Her change of clothes had been carefully selected, all were easy to step in and out of without assistance.

In her room, at the rear of the inn, she was unaware of the arrival of the second coach and did not hear the angry altercation that took place in the vestibule when the owner discovered there were no suitable rooms available for himself that night.

Chapter Two

HESTER WOKE WHEN Birdie brought her morning chocolate. She sat up, rubbing her eyes, disorientated. 'What time is it? I feel as though I've only been asleep for an hour or two.'

'It's after seven o'clock, my dear, and I thought it wise to rouse you early. There are things you need to *know*.'

She was wide awake. 'Tell me, have you heard why Aunt Agatha would not let us in yesterday?' She raised a hand as her companion prepared to put the tray across her knees. 'No, Birdie, put it on the side table. I shall get up. There's something awry, or you would not be here so early *and* fully clothed.'

With her companion's assistance she was soon dressed in yesterday's costume, freshly sponged and pressed by an obliging chambermaid. She sat down in front of the mirror and impatiently gathered up her hair into its usual chignon and pinned it securely to her head.

'My dear, despite your lack of sleep you look pretty as a picture. I've always said that autumn colours suit your nut-brown hair. It's a pity you have to hide your outfit under that ugly cloak.'

Hester was now intrigued. Why was Birdie taking such an the interest in her appearance? 'Birdie, tell me why I have to look my best this morning? Who am I to impress?'

She watched as Miss Bird walked her measured way across

the rag rug to stand gazing pensively at the fire. She knew not to interrupt whilst her erstwhile governess, and now dearest friend, was considering her next utterance. While she waited, she rose from her seat in front of the mirror and walked to the window, peeping out from between the heavy curtains to see it was, as expected, still dark.

Her friend turned, her face serious. 'After you retired to your room I decided to go downstairs and sit in the snug. A woman of my sort is often overlooked and indeed, such was the case last night.' She indicated that Hester should be seated in the small armchair beside the fire.

'The place was in fine uproar. Everyone was talking about it. It seems the occupant of the coach in front of us yesterday was a Lord Colebrook, the Earl of Waverly. It is his dust we were following for two hours. It seems he was not best pleased to find we had bespoken the only decent chambers.'

Hester couldn't help smiling; she had no love for aristocrats of any description; if she was honest, her sympathies had lain, like those of her aunt, more with the sanculottes, the revolutionaries in France. Of course, beheading all the aristocrats had not been a pretty solution, but she believed the poor deserved better from their masters. She contained her curiosity and waited to hear the remainder of Birdie's story.

'Mr Jarvis was ordered to turn us out and give us the inferior rooms but, bless him, he refused. He insisted that gentry or not, ladies came first in his opinion. The general consensus was that his lordship was not pleased. However, by the time I arrived the altercation was over and the gentleman in question was sitting over a large jug of claret nursing his woes.'

Hester couldn't restrain herself. 'He sounds typical of his class. I'm glad he had to spend the night in meagre accommodation. Now, tell me immediately, what manner of man is he? Is his appearance as repellent as his nature?'

'Well, he's an extremely tall man, wide-shouldered and brown-haired. I wouldn't call him handsome, but he has a striking appearance. Actually, he has the demeanour of a soldier, a man more used to commanding troops than arguing with a landlord in a country hostelry.'

'Because he shouted? In my limited experience the rich and influential are prone to do so when thwarted. Do you know exactly what their rooms were like?'

'I'm coming to that, my dear. After it became apparent that the landlord was not going to budge and we were to remain, the gentleman and his companion, a more common-looking individual, presumably his valet, took themselves off to discuss matters. Which is why they were in the snug in the first place.'

'I wonder why someone so toplofty as the Earl of Waverly was also visiting Neddingfield Hall? I don't suppose you overheard them discussing why the gates were barred?'

Miss Bird shook her head. 'I did not, my dear. However, taproom gossip, according to Tom, is that that your aunt and her staff are definitely in residence. They have to pass through the town in order to leave.'

'How odd! But you know my aunt, she's a law unto herself. I think she's about to embark on one of her extraordinary adventures and wishes to inform me of it.'

If this was the case it didn't explain why a member of the nobility should also be visiting. It wasn't a coincidence: Aunt Agatha must have had a reason for asking them both to come at the same time. A thought popped, unbidden, into her head. She almost choked, spraying her chocolate in a most unladylike manner across the boards. Coughing and spluttering, she leapt to her feet, incapable of explaining to her companion what had discommoded her.

When she recovered her composure she was able to say in an

almost natural tone what she suspected. 'I think I know why this Lord Colebrook is here. Aunt Agatha has decided it's time I married and has invited him along to make me an offer. Perhaps she thinks I will renege on the promise to attend the season this year.'

She waited for an explosion of laughter, for Birdie's vehement denial of her outrageous statement but none was forthcoming. Instead, her friend's expression changed from one of alarm to amusement.

'Of course! How silly of me not to have thought of that. Last time we visited, dear Miss Culley and I had a comfortable coze whilst you were gallivanting around the countryside on your horse; she confided to me that she had exactly the man for you and would arrange for you to meet. She decided that, as you're approaching two and twenty it was high time you gave up your single state.'

'Birdie! How could you? A lady is supposed to marry to better herself or her family, but I've no need to do that. I've told you countless times, matrimony is not for me. My two dearest friends both believed themselves to be in love and embarked on the married state. Look at them now! Poor Charlotte is at daggers drawn with Sir Charles and from what I gather from her last letter, she has banished him to the dower house.'

Birdie chuckled. 'Yes, and Miss Merryweather, now Lady Alsop, is about to produce her fourth bundle of delight in as many years. From one extreme to the other, my dear. I know you have no wish to emulate them, but your mama begged me to keep you safe and guide you to a happier life than she had.'

Hester felt her eyes filling at the mention of her mother. It was true; her papa had been neither a good husband nor father. He had been a weak man and his answer to every problem was to give in to it, eventually giving in to a bout of pneumonia when, as Mama had remarked on the morning of his funeral, *'If your father had had any backbone he would have fought the disease and recovered and not left us to manage on our own.'*

'Whatever my father's failings – and they were legion, I will admit this to no one but yourself, Birdie – he didn't waste my inheritance; neither Mama nor I ever went without. I have sufficient money in the funds to keep me in whatever style I choose for the remainder of my life. Why should I wish to give that up?'

'Why indeed? There's no need for you to do anything you don't want, my dear. Your aunt and I merely discussed the hope that you would meet someone your equal in both intelligence and wit and decide that being a spinster was no longer the best option. Surely, child, you would like to have children one day?'

Hester swirled around the floor, the heavy woollen skirts of her dress impeding her long strides. She stopped, glaring down at the offending garment and came to a decision.

'This is ridiculous. Help me change into my riding habit, please. I shall take Tom and James and ride to the far side of the park. We can get into Neddingfield by fording the river. Although it's cold it hasn't rained for weeks and it should be quite safe to cross.'

'Is it your intention to discover what Miss Culley has in mind, before you're obliged to meet the gentleman?'

Hester nodded as she flung her gown on to the bed. 'You think it's a good idea, don't you, Birdie? I promise, if he's suitable, apart from the fact that he sounds arrogant and autocratic, I shall be civil to him and not turn him down without a fair hearing.'

It was scarcely dawn when Hester was cantering away from the inn. She was determined to speak to her aunt before his lordship arrived to look down his nose at her. She glanced down at the black shape loping along beside her; at least Jet was delighted with the excursion as was Thunder. She could feel his muscles bunching and releasing beneath her; in spite of his long journey yesterday he was eager and ready to go.

She led the way through the town, around several farms and down various back lanes, her visual memory excellent. She believed this was the only worthwhile thing she'd inherited from her father. She sat back in the saddle, pulling gently on the reins and her horse responded immediately, dropping back to a trot and then to a long, easy walk. Whilst she waited for her henchmen to catch up she had time to reconsider the sketchy information she had about her adversary.

'Tom, if we go down this path we shall arrive at the river. If I remember rightly all we need to do then is follow the bank for about half a mile until we reach a bend in the river where we can ford.'

'I'm glad you waited until light to set off, Miss Frobisher. I wouldn't like to do this ride in the dark.'

'Did you doubt me, Tom?'

The man shook his head, his face serious. 'No, miss, but I'm not sure creeping about the countryside is the best approach.'

'Would you have preferred me to have waited patiently at the inn until I discovered why my aunt barred the gates?' He nodded and Hester's laugh echoed through the naked trees, sending a flock of pigeons into the air. The flapping startled Thunder and for the next few moments she was fully occupied calming him and the conversation was forgotten.

She was delighted to discover the crossing place was exactly where she thought it would be. They reined in and she eyed the grey swirling water with disfavour. 'It looks a lot deeper than I anticipated. It must have been raining for the river to be so full.'

'I'll try it, miss. You wait on the bank with James.' She watched Tom push his mount forward, knowing it was right he discover if the crossing was safe. Hester held her breath as he urged the nervous animal down, she could hear the horses' hoofs striking the gravel bed of the river.

The water swirled about the animal's hocks, then rose almost to Tom's stirrup irons. She thought he would be forced to turn back and knew she would be disappointed if he did. Then to her relief the water became shallower and Tom was safely across. He patted the chestnut's neck; it was Bess, one of the carriage horses, who went as well under saddle as she did leading a team.

'It's safe, Miss Frobisher, it looks deeper than it is. If you come next, James can ride behind, that way Thunder can't change his mind.'

Hester smiled. She knew he was recalling the embarrassing occasion when her horse had been halfway across a narrow bridge and balked, refusing to go further. In the end she had been forced to dismount and back him across the bridge, much to the amusement of James and Tom who had crossed ahead of her.

She dug her heel into his side and, slapping him on the neck, urged him into the foaming water. Jet chose that precise moment to erupt from the undergrowth and fling himself into the river with a splash. Being suddenly deluged in icy water so startled them both that she and Thunder parted company. She landed on her back in the river. Thunder, half-rearing, lunged forward to join Tom on the far bank.

The water was barely two feet deep, but for a terrifying moment it closed over her head and she could see nothing except swirling blackness above. Then an arm reached down and she was hauled to the surface coughing, spluttering and freezing cold.

James was standing beside her, the water not even over his boot tops, trying hard to keep a straight face. She glared at him, daring him to comment on her misfortune. Without waiting to have her stupid horse brought back she stomped across the river; after all she was so wet, what would a little more water matter?

With some difficulty she was assisted back into the saddle, her riding habit clinging unpleasantly to her legs, and even with Tom's cloak around her shivering miserably. Through chattering teeth she called, 'Tom, let's get to the Hall. It's not far through the park. I keep fresh garments there and I'm sure James can borrow something from one of the grooms.'

She led the way through the woods, the area becoming more familiar, and she saw the park ahead. 'I'm going to gallop the rest of the way, Tom, it will warm us both up.' She kicked her mount and he responded. They raced across the frost-whitened grass arriving by the tradesman's entrance.

Not waiting to be assisted from the saddle she flung herself down and turned to throw the reins to a stable boy. The yard was deserted, the cobbles unswept, the stable block empty. Where was everyone? Puzzled, she called out, receiving no response.

The clatter of her retainers arriving was welcome, James could take care of the horses and Tom could accompany her. This was decidedly odd – first the barred gates and now the abandoned yard. The sooner she got inside and saw for herself what was going on the better.

'Tom, come with me. I must get indoors before I freeze to death.'

'I'm not sure we should go any further, miss. It's right strange, the yard being empty. Where's everyone gone? They can't have left, or someone would have seen them.' He glanced around nervously. 'I don't like this. Something's not right. Best we go back to the inn.'

'No, Tom, certainly not. I've no idea where everyone is, but I intend to find out and I won't do that standing around here in sodden clothes.'

She set off at a run, her skirts flapping uncomfortably around her water-filled boots. The flagged path led from the stable block, past the outbuildings used as laundry and dairy, along the barn and up to the rear of the enormous building. She knew at once that something was amiss. The shutters were closed on the upstairs windows and no smoke was belching from the chimneys. The place was as uninhabited as the stables.

'My aunt's obviously away from home. However, I must gain entrance. I know where the key to the scullery door is hidden. God willing it will still be there and we can get in. I can find clothes to change into and you can kindle the kitchen range and boil a kettle.'

Her priority was to get warm – she would worry about the mysterious disappearance of her aunt and her staff when that was accomplished.

Chapter Three

THE KEY WAS hanging in the laundry outbuilding where Hester had sent Tom to look and she stamped her feet as he unlocked the scullery door. Shivering, she stumbled inside the house glad to get out of bitter November wind.

'Good heavens! It's almost as cold inside as out. Tom, go to the kitchens and light the range. I shall use the back stairs to my apartment and hope that by the time I return there will be a hot drink awaiting me.'

She headed for the servant's staircase clutching her heavy skirts in one hand and a hastily lit candlestick in the other. The winding steps led directly to the first floor upon which the main bedrooms were all located.

Knowing her way about the house made it easier for her to arrive at the correct door without getting lost in the rabbit warren of passages. She felt sorry for any staff who had to nego-tiate them carrying trays and brimming chamber pots.

She emerged, a little warmer from her exertions, in the wide carpeted corridor that ran the length of the building. Crossing quickly to her chambers, she entered, eager to find dry clothes. It was strange going in with the shutters closed, and the shrouded furniture made the familiar sitting-room look strange. Good gracious! The holland covers were on! This meant that her aunt had definitely not been expecting her. Whatever was going on? Why had she been sent the letter?

Deciding it would be better to leave this question unanswered until she was dry, she hurried into her dressing-room. Mercifully it was slightly warmer in there as it only had one outside wall and a small window. Stripping off her clothes, she stood naked on a square of linen taken from the shelf and rubbed herself dry. Then she wound her dripping hair in another towel and twisted it on top of her head in a makeshift turban.

Stretching out, she removed clean undergarments from a pile, glad she had had the foresight to keep several changes of raiment here. They might be out-dated, but they were warm and serviceable; unless she needed new clothes she was content to wear what she already owned.

However, she'd recently replenished her wardrobe, ready for the season, having promised both Aunt Agatha and Birdie that she would, just this once, parade around the *ton*, in the remote hope that she might meet someone with whom she could contemplate spending the rest of her life.

Relieved her teeth had stopped clattering, her hands no longer blue, in chemise and petticoats she stepped smartly across to the closet and opened the doors. She chose a warm woollen gown, high-necked and long-sleeved, exactly what she needed. Its saving grace was the colour – a rich russet, which brought out the chestnut gleams in her hair. Snatching up a warm cashmere shawl from a shelf she spread it around her shoulders and immediately felt better. All she had to do now was find stockings and slippers and she would be ready to go and investigate.

Deciding to retrace her steps, as it was far quicker than going down the main staircase and across the enormous parquet entrance hall, she picked up the candle and left through the door in her dressing-room. She, paused momentarily at the bottom of the back stairs to release her skirts before pushing open the door.

She froze. There were strangers outside. Her hand remained in mid-air, inches away from the door. She held her breath, praying she wouldn't be discovered.

Lord Colebrook stiffened, his eyes narrowed, aware of some-thing a civilian would not have detected. His years serving as an officer in Wellington's army had honed his senses to a fine degree. His quick reflexes and keen hearing had saved himself and his men from certain death on several occasions in the past. He gestured to Robin, his ex-sergeant major, to continue talking as though nothing untoward was happening. The man took his cue, as he always did.

'Well, the thing is, my lord, I can't think where Miss Culley can be. She certainly isn't here and neither are any of her staff.'

By this time Ralph was standing beside the servants' stairs. He could see the door was open a fraction. Someone was lurking behind it and that someone was about to receive an unpleasant surprise.

His arms shot out, one hand grabbing the door, flinging it wide, whilst the other reached in and grabbed the intruder by the throat, throwing him across the passageway where he crashed unconscious to the floor.

He realized as soon as he'd released his grip that he'd made a dreadful mistake. The intruder wasn't a man, but a lovely young woman with wavy chestnut brown hair, and she lay spread-eagled on the floor, possibly fatally injured by his foolhardy actions.

'Bloody hell! What have I done?' In one stride he was across the corridor, dropping to his knees beside her. Expertly he ran his hands down her limbs to check for breaks, relieved to find they were intact. She was so still, so cold; for a heart-stopping moment he thought he had broken her neck.

Gently he slid his hands along her shoulders, cradling her

head between his calloused fingers. He traced the vertebrae, checking each was in place and, as he did so he became aware that his hands were not around a corpse, he could feel a slow, but rhythmic, pulse beneath his fingers.

'Thank God! She's alive. And her neck's not broken. She's unconscious, but I pray not seriously injured.'

His exclamation still hung in the air when he heard a roar of rage from further down the corridor. Too late he glanced up to see himself staring down the barrel of a pistol held by a man with murder in his eyes. Not for the first time he knew he was looking death in the face. He knew better than to move a muscle. He merely raised his eyes to hold the stranger's attention.

'The young lady's not seriously harmed, merely unconscious.'

He could feel Robin rigid beside him and knew the matter hung in the balance. He could hardly protest his innocence, for he had thrown the girl against the wall himself. He swallowed, maybe this time his luck *had* run out. He knew for a certainty that if this lovely young woman had been his love, *he* would not hesitate to kill the man who had caused her harm.

He dropped his hands and spoke again, his tone unthreatening. 'May I stand up? If I'm to meet my Maker, I would prefer to do it upright, not on my knees.' His prosaic speech seemed to register with his assailant; he saw the man's fury abating.

'What happened here? How's Miss Frobisher injured? I heard her crash against the wall and she didn't get there by tripping, that's for sure.'

Ralph felt his stomach clench and its contents threaten to return. Could matters get any worse? This was not some stranger he had injured, but a young woman who had as much right as he to be wandering about here.

'God! What a bloody awful catastrophe! Look, could you put that pistol down; you're making me nervous? If you don't intend to shoot me, allow me to introduce myself.'

The pistol was lowered, but held ready, as the man waited for an explanation.

Ralph half bowed. 'I'm Ralph Sinclair that was, now Lord Colebrook, the Earl of Waverly. I believe that this must be Hester Frobisher, my distant cousin. Miss Agatha Culley is my great aunt as well as hers.'

Hester became aware of voices speaking above her. She felt as though she had been thrown from her horse, and her head hurt abominably. For a moment she kept her eyes closed, trying to make sense of the world. She was obviously lying on the floor; she could feel the cold of uncarpeted boards seeping through her clothes.

Should she risk a peep? If she glanced through her lashes whoever it was might not realize she was awake. She had been attacked, so it would be well to continue to feign unconsciousness. All she could see were a pair of riding boots, extremely large ones. Whoever owned these must be a prodigiously tall gentleman. Slowly her head cleared and she was aware that the wearer of the boots was talking. What he said slowly filtered into her muddled senses.

Quite forgetting she was supposed to be unaware she attempted to sit upright, but the effort proved too much and her head spun. She sunk back clutching her forehead, unable to hold back the gasp of pain.

Instantly Lord Colebrook was at her side and, without asking permission, slipped his arms under her knees and shoulders and lifted her easily. She felt too sick and dizzy to protest. She was outraged that the man who had caused her hurt was acting as her saviour. She remembered quite clearly the moment of terror as a grip of iron had circled her neck and thrown her head first into the wall. This man was a brute, almost a murderer. Perhaps it was he who had done away with Aunt Agatha. These were her last coherent thoughts before a whirling blackness enveloped her for a second time.

Ralph decided it would be too cumbersome to attempt the narrow stairs the servants used whilst carrying an unconscious girl, so he turned and bounded back down the corridor, out into the grand hall taking the wide oak stairs two at a time. He remembered, from previous visits, which apartment Miss Frobisher used. His great aunt had indicated their whereabouts and told him about the girl, although until today he had never had the pleasure of making her acquaintance. If he had known how beautiful she was he might have been less reluctant to meet her.

He smiled grimly; he had hardly endeared himself to her by his monstrous treatment. He shouldered his way into her private sitting-room. God, it was cold as ice everywhere in this barracks of a house.

'Robin, go downstairs and find something to light a fire in her bedroom. I'm sure between you, you can rustle up something to burn. If you can't find any fuel, use a chair.'

He supposed he shouldn't be entering a lady's bedchamber, but needs must. He was uncomfortably aware that the man with the pistol was shadowing him, a hand's breadth from his shoulder at all times; obviously a retainer of some sort, who didn't trust him as far as he could spit.

'Quick, man, check if the bed is damp. If it is, I'll wrap her in that comforter and rest her on the day-bed in front of the fire.' The man didn't argue, just stepped round him.

'The bed's no good, my lord.' Ralph watched him remove the comforter holding it to his cheek. 'This will do. I'll fetch that *chaise-longue* over. I reckon there's enough kindling to start the fire, and some coal left in the scuttle.' The man's expression lightened a trifle as he added, 'And if there isn't, I'll smash a chair or two, shall I?'

Ralph stood patiently holding the girl, her face resting against his shoulder and couldn't help noticing the length of her black lashes and the way they curled enticingly at the ends. What colour had her eyes been? He'd only glimpsed them for a second before she'd collapsed. He rather thought they were a mixture of green and brown, like his own, a perfect complement to her hair, which lay in abundant tresses around her shoulders. It was only then he became aware that her hair was wet.

'Why's Miss Frobisher's hair wet?'

The man, scrabbling away with the tinderbox in the fender, answered without looking up from his task. 'She fell in the river on the way over here, my lord.'

Everything about this trip was baffling. Ralph shook his head. First the urgent summons to come to Neddingfield Hall, then the barred gates, the lack of accommodation at the Jug and Bottle, and finally discovering an unknown relative playing hide and go seek on the stairs.

Where the hell was Aunt Agatha? The place was under covers, and there was no sign of recent occupation in the kitchen either. He hadn't had time to search more than the downstairs rooms. He would need to examine his aunt's chambers and discover what kind of clothes she had taken with her, as it was possible this might give him a clue to her whereabouts. However, it didn't give him the slightest inkling as to why he'd been summoned to this place when his relative was absent.

He heard the welcome sound of crackling in the grate. 'Good man. Now, drag the day-bed over. Shall I lay Miss Frobisher down and help you?'

'I can manage, sir.'

Five minutes later Ralph was able to deposit his burden, mummified in the warm comforter, on to the makeshift bed in front of the meagre fire. He looked round for something else to burn and on discovering two wicker laundry baskets in the dressing-room he smashed them and piled them in the grate. Soon the room was warm, and Ralph felt it was safe to leave the injured girl in the charge of her manservant.

'You didn't give me your name; how am I to address you?'

The man nodded briefly. 'I'm Tom Clark, my lord. I'm Miss Frobisher's man of business, so to speak.'

'Very well, Tom Clark, I shall leave you to attend your mistress. Where is her maidservant, her companion?' His wits were wandering, his needle sharp intellect not functioning. 'Presumably Miss Frobisher's companion, the one she was travelling with, is back at the hostelry? Is there someone I can send to fetch her here?'

'You can, my lord, but she'll not be able to come; she doesn't ride, and the carriage can't come through closed gates.'

'They're no longer barred: we scaled the gates and undid them.'

For the first time Ralph saw the man's mouth bend; he was obviously impressed by the fact that the massive cast-iron gates had been opened by just the two of them.

'That's great news, my lord. James is downstairs – you can send him. Miss Bird will be here with all the trappings in no time at all. There's a quack in the town as well – should James fetch him?'

'Yes. Miss Frobisher obviously has a concussion, but the fact that she regained consciousness, even briefly, is a good sign.'

For some reason he was reluctant to leave the bedchamber; he wanted to stay and watch the girl, see the gentle rise and fall of her chest, be certain she was breathing. He strode back downstairs to find Robin on his way up with an armful of logs and a broad smile.

'The range is going, my lord. The kettle's on the hob, and young James has found the makings for tea and a decent bottle of brandy.'

'Make sure Clark has sufficient fuel to keep the room warm, and light a fire in her parlour as well, then come back to the kitchen.'

He found a young man of medium build, a shock of corn-coloured hair and no boots. The stranger was busy warming bricks to take up. Ralph was relieved that he hadn't had to go outside to find James. He had a bad feeling about this; every instinct told him there was danger – but from what he wasn't certain, but he was damn sure he was going to find out.

'You must be James. I want you to get back to town and fetch Miss Bird; also, get someone from the inn to find the doctor and have him attend here.'

The young man nodded. 'Yes, sir, I mean, my lord.'

So used to commanding men Ralph hardly noticed the speed with which the servant moved to replace his boots. It was what he expected: it was a brave man indeed who dared to ignore his orders.

Chapter Four

'M Y DEAR GIRL, YOUR sickness *will* pass and the headache lessen. Dr Radcliff assured me that although you have a concussion, it's not a serious one. You'll be up and about in a day or so.'

Hester flopped back on the pillows, closing her eyes to allow the waves of nausea to subside; no sooner had she swallowed something, it seemed to her, than she cast up her accounts. And it was all the fault of that monster, that arrogant aristocrat, because for some reason he had taken it upon himself to treat her as a common criminal.

'Now, have a little sip of boiled water, my dear, it will take the nasty taste away.'

She turned her head, childishly refusing the drink. She heard Birdie sigh and knew she was a sore trial to her. At this moment she felt too wretched to apologize. She heard the sound of someone attending the fire, but didn't bother to turn her head to discover who it was.

Presumably the mysterious vanishing act accomplished by the staff here had been reversed and with the touch of his aristocratic hand Lord Colebrook had restored things to normal. No doubt the place was teeming with eager servants, Aunt Agatha returned to her apartments, and everything as it should be.

She dozed, letting her thoughts wander. She found that if she kept her head still, especially after the bouts of sickness, the headache was not as bad and her thoughts not as jumbled. She listened to the muted conversation on the far side of the room and what she overheard forced her to pay attention.

'Robin, are you sure about that?' Birdie was asking, her voice alarmed. 'Miss Culley left Neddingfield without taking her things with her?'

His reply was quiet. 'Absolutely certain, Miss Bird. His lordship and I have gone through her apartments carefully. The trunks are still in the attic, so if she's taken any clothes, then it was in a carpet bag. Also she hasn't taken her spyglass or carriage clock. His lordship says his aunt never travels without *them*.'

Miss Culley was Lord Colebrook's aunt? How could that be? As far as she knew Aunt Agatha only had two relatives living, herself and Ralph Sinclair. Where had this Lord Colebrook sprung from?

The import of the information she had heard before this revelation finally registered. Her aunt never travelled without her spyglass and clock and always took two or three trunks. She would never have gone away in such a manner. Something awful had happened and Hester was lying half dead, unable to investigate. It was all the fault of the man whose valet was tending to her fire.

From somewhere she found the strength to push herself upright on the pillows. She waited until her head stopped pounding before attempting to open her eyes. Birdie had her back to her, was standing to one side of the fire whilst a man, in a serviceable brown jacket, did what was necessary in the grate.

'Excuse me, Robin, or whatever your name is, I wish to speak to you.' Her voice emerged somewhat louder than she'd expected.

The man crouching at the fireplace was so startled by her peremptory command he tumbled backwards sending the ashes from his bucket and shovel spiralling into the air. The resulting coughing and choking would have been amusing if it hadn't added to her own discomfort. Eventually the air cleared and the final particles of grey were swept away. Birdie came over smiling fondly at Hester.

'I'm delighted you're feeling better, my dear. Poor Robin's most upset that he covered us both in ash. He says he will come back later to speak to you, but has duties elsewhere at the moment.'

'Botheration. Well, maybe you can find the information I need. I heard him say Aunt Agatha is also this Lord Colebrook's aunt. As far as I know the only relative she has, apart from myself, is Ralph Sinclair, and he is no more an aristocrat than I am.' She watched her companion's eyes twinkle. 'What is it, Birdie? What are you not telling me?'

'They are one and the same, my dear. I discovered that soon after I arrived yesterday. Your cousin, albeit a very distant one, inherited a fortune and an earldom, from an even more distant uncle. It seems that your Aunt Agatha didn't know about this relative; the connection was so thin as to be almost non-existent. However, there was a direct link through the male line down to the gentleman in question.'

'I don't understand anything any more, Birdie. Two days ago we were planning the opening of our townhouse; I was eagerly anticipating attending the opera, theatre and visiting the museums. Now here I am cruelly injured by an ennobled relative, and my aunt mysteriously disappeared, along with all her staff.'

Birdie patted her hand. 'Never mind, my dear. You were bemoaning the lack of excitement in your life only the other week.'

Hester could hear her friend chuckling as she walked back across the bedroom to pull the window closed now the air was clear.

*

Ralph was sitting at the scrubbed kitchen table, a steaming cup of coffee clasped between his hands. He glanced up, perplexed, to observe Robin was covered in ash and rather pink about the cheeks.

'Good God! Can't you manage a simple task like clearing a grate without disaster, Robin?'

'I beg your pardon, my lord, Miss Frobisher startled me and I dropped the bucket. Her companion and the room are in a worse state than I.'

Ralph was on his feet immediately. 'She's awake? Is she well enough for me to speak to her? I have yet to make my grovelling apologies, and explain how I came to treat her so roughly.'

'No, my lord. I believe she heard Miss Bird and I talking about your aunt and it was the news of her having left the premises without her normal baggage that caused Miss Frobisher to call out.'

'Dammit! The poor girl has had enough to cope with this past twenty-four hours, I don't want her worrying unnecessarily about that.' He settled back in his chair and resumed his morose staring. The more he discovered the less he understood.

His first concern must be the well-being of the two ladies unexpectedly in his charge. He had sent Clark into town to find some temporary staff to run the place. With the parlous state of employment in rural areas such as these, he hoped there might be several families with members eager to come, even if their employment was not to be permanent.

'Robin, has Clark returned? I'm hoping he will have arranged for the servants we need.'

There was no need for Robin to answer as he heard Tom come in the rear porch banging his boots noisily and pausing long enough to hang up his riding coat before entering.

'Good news, my lord. I went to the inn and asked if word be sent out to anyone seeking employment in the area. I managed to engage a dozen women within twenty minutes and half-a-dozen men to work outside; they are on their way as I speak.'

'I hope there will be someone who can cook amongst them. Robin has exhausted his repertoire of recipes and hungry as I was this morning, even I could not manage to swallow his attempt at bread.'

'Yes, there's an older lady, and her daughter, who come highly recommended.' Tom walked over to the range and poured himself a cup of coffee before joining him at the table.

'That was the good news, sir. However, there's been a tragedy. It seems that a local lady died yesterday.' Ralph raised a quizzical eyebrow. 'I know it seems hardly our business, my lord, but from what I hear the lady was returning home in a state of fear because of what she had heard about Neddingfield. The talk is of spirits and ghosts; that the disappearance and the accidents have been caused by supernatural means. The poor lady frightened herself to death; her heart gave up under the strain.'

'Sad, but hardly my concern. Gossips always exaggerate, you know that. Before long we will have mass hysteria all round and some interfering busybody will call out the militia.' He swallowed the last mouthful of coffee and straightened. 'I've sent young James out to reconnoitre the area, see if he can find sign of men being in the vicinity over the past few days. I'm going to have a closer look round the barns and outbuildings. Robin, you and Clark come with me.'

He shrugged on his coat, not waiting to see if they were following; he knew they were. The outbuildings contained the usual paraphernalia one would expect in such an establishment. The carriage house was full; neither the chaise nor the antiquated coach missing. Good God! His wits were wandering.

'Robin, where are the carriage horses? In fact, where are any of the horses? The chickens, ducks, and farmyard cats are here, but no dogs or horses. What does that suggest to you?' Impatiently he stared at his ex-sergeant-major hoping he would also recognize the clues. 'Dammit, man, think. How many times did we see villages left in just this way? The people vanished into thin air, horses and dogs gone too?'

Enlightenment dawned. 'I have it. It's as though the place has been evacuated; they must have left on horseback, presumably in the middle of the night, as nobody local heard or saw anything. That must be why your aunt took so little baggage, only what she could carry.'

'But why did they take the dogs along? It doesn't make sense.'

He looked round the empty yard. There was something here that didn't quite fit this scenario. What was common on the Peninsular when the French were rapidly approaching a Spanish village did not explain why Neddingfield should have been abandoned in the same way. Neither did it explain why Aunt Agatha had sent an urgent note to himself and Miss Frobisher to visit and then not waited for them to arrive.

He kicked angrily at a chicken pecking his feet and it squawked, bustling off, its outrage obvious in every cluck. He was on his way back to the house when he heard the sound of a horse galloping towards them and paused. No one arrived pell-mell unless the news was urgent.

The animal thundered into the yard and its rider, James, dragged it to a halt. He vaulted from the saddle and, dropping the reins casually in front of the horse, ran across the yard.

'I've found something, my lord. And it's not good, I can tell you. There are signs that at least a dozen, possibly more, men were camping at the far side of the park, but there's something strange about it. Gave me the shivers. The camp's empty now, but I reckon it was occupied not long ago.'

Ralph turned angrily to Tom. 'Why did you hear none of this

in town, Clark? Surely such a large band of strangers must have been noticed by someone and the two things linked to what's going on here?'

The man flushed, whether from annoyance or embarrassment Ralph neither knew nor cared. 'I beg your pardon, my lord, I only arrived here myself yesterday. I've been somewhat busy since then, what with my mistress being attacked and every-thing.'

Ralph felt his cheeks redden and raised a placating hand. 'I apologize. I have no right to roar at you. It's my own stupidity that's led to this. First I take my cousin for an intruder and then fail to do the most basic of information gathering.' He shrugged, before turning to speak to Robin. 'The fact that men were camped …' He swung back to James. 'Are you certain that it was not a Romany encampment? Did you see evidence of women or children?'

'No, my lord. That was the first thing I thought myself. It looked a very professional setup, everything set out neat like and proper rails to tether their mounts. But there was no sign there'd been any wagons at the place.' James shook his head, his mouth twisting. 'There's something odd about it; you'll under-stand what I mean when you see for yourself, my lord.'

'Can you find your way back there? I think in spite of my reservations, it's time to call out the militia. God's teeth! How I wish I had my chosen men with me now. We could flush out the buggers easily enough then.'

He saddled Thunder, the only mount up to his weight. He cursed the fact he had not had the foresight to bring his stallion with him. He stopped beside his coach to retrieve his pistols from the side pocket, checking they were primed and loaded, then tucked them into the deep pockets of his riding coat.

'Lead the way, James. We shall follow.'

Ralph was relieved that Miss Frobisher's man had visited

Neddingfield before and knew his way around the park and ancient woods. But even so he doubted they would have found their way back to the camp if James hadn't left a trail wide enough for a blind man to follow. As they cantered across the greensward, Ralph was pleasantly surprised by the quality of the horse he was riding. That it was a thoroughbred was obvious from its conformation, but the animal was also well schooled and obedient to the bit; in fact, it was far too good for a girl.

Twenty minutes' hard riding brought them to the coastal side of the park, an area rarely frequented by gamekeepers or poachers. He guessed the paths he observed had been made by smugglers after they'd landed their goods. Since the end of hostilities with France this illegal trade in contraband had increased and in spite of the government appointing more militia and customs officers to protect their shores the nefarious trade flourished.

He smiled wryly as he remembered drinking a fine brandy the previous night – no doubt it too had arrived without taxes being paid, like much of the claret hidden away in the wine cellars under Neddingfield.

James raised his hand, indicating they were to slacken their pace. They must be at their destination. He eased back on the reins, as did Robin who was riding beside him. Tom Clark was ahead, riding beside his friend. Ralph rather feared he had made an enemy of him.

The young man halted and swung to the ground. 'I think it's best if we tie the horses here; I'd like you to see the encampment as I did, my lord.'

'It's possible I can establish how many men there were by the evidence they've left. It might also be possible to say which way they travelled, and if they were accompanied.' He didn't need to elucidate, the others knew he was referring to the missing staff and owner of Neddingfield.

His men stepped aside, allowing him to walk ahead. He pushed some overhanging branches aside and found himself standing on the edge of what could have been an abandoned camp left by soldiers. James was right to think it had a military flavour; in fact, he didn't have to look around the enclosure to know the men who had been here were ex-soldiers. However, what they were doing camping in this remote place, or what they had to do with his aunt, he had no notion.

He remained on the outside of the clearing and the others stood and waited for instructions. He frowned. There was something about this place unsettling him. He could see the imprints of horses hoofs, but something was missing. God's teeth! There were no footprints, none at all. He felt the hairs on the back of his neck stand up and he shivered involuntarily. He glanced over his shoulder to see if the others had seen it. There'd been too much talk of ghosts and goblins, and he had no intention of fuelling speculation. This was an observation he would keep to himself.

'Robin, go and see if you can count how many horses they had tethered over there. Tom, you and James walk along the small paths on that side. See if any of them show signs of having been used recently.'

He stood in the middle of the clearing counting the sleeping hollows. He pushed his fanciful notions to the back of his mind. He was a soldier. He dealt with facts. There were seventeen spaces on one side of the fire, two on the other. He imagined these were for the equivalent of officers, the rest the rank-and-file. There was something else that bothered him. The place was too clean, no troops he'd ever commanded left their camp looking so tidy. Where was the detritus that always accompanied such a place?

He kicked viciously at a flat stone left in the fire pit and the pain of his stubbed toe cleared his head. It was one disaster after the other at the moment. First he had had this wretched title foisted on him and the fortune and responsibilities that went with it. He was a simple man, a professional soldier; he'd never accumulated possessions. The bounty he'd won in his many campaigns had been invested in the funds, and he was comfortable, but not wealthy.

He knew, like his cousin, he stood to inherit half his aunt's fortune when she died, but, as she'd told him several times over the past few years, he was more likely to predecease her, the kind of rackety life he lived. He had almost perished on several occasions, and had the scars to prove it.

But when his lawyers eventually tracked him down to inform him he was in direct line to inherit an earldom and three estates he had been dumbfounded. What did he need with all that responsibility?

Since his return from France with the Duke of Wellington, he had bought himself a smart house in Brook Street, and was quite content to spend his days drinking and gambling with his friends, or staying at house parties all over the country. He knew he was invited because he was a hero of Waterloo; Major Sinclair had been mentioned in dispatches, and had a string of impressive medals to pin to his regimentals to prove it.

His lawyer was following the trail of another distant branch of the family, cousins of Aunt Agatha's. He had not given up hope someone else might yet be found and he would be able to relinquish this unwanted grandeur and all the bother that went with it. His despondent thoughts were interrupted by a shout from Tom.

'Over here, my lord, we've found something.'

Chapter Five

'MY LORD, LOOK at this.'

He looked and his eyes narrowed. The path at this point was overgrown with hawthorn bushes and hanging from a patch of vicious thorns was a strip of red material. Ralph realized it was from the jacket of a soldier. This was something tangible, not like the campsite; for a while he'd been unnerved, beginning to suspect he was dealing with the supernatural.

'God's teeth! A group of ex-soldiers masquerading as serving members? This band of renegades must have convinced my aunt to accompany them.' Whoever was behind this had money and brains – this was not the work of an amateur.

'Shall I follow the trail, my lord? I'm not sure where it goes; I've visited here several times, but I've never been to this part before.'

'Do that. I'm convinced they can't have taken them far. It would be nigh on impossible to keep their passage secret. Travel carefully, keep your heads down and if you see anything suspicious observe, don't get embroiled in something you can't handle on your own.'

The men returned with him to retrieve their horses and he watched them mount and head off, single file, through the gap. The coast lay in that direction, and with luck they would be back in an hour or so. Robin joined him by the empty fire-pit and

Ralph sensed his disquiet; perhaps it would be wise to leave before his man noticed the lack of human footprints.

'I've seen enough here, it's time I returned. I still have to make my peace with my cousin.'

Hester, feeling considerably better, was able to eat a slice of dry toast and drink a dish of weak tea without any unpleasant after-effects. Birdie had gone downstairs to see if she could find writing materials in the study. If they were to be staying here for more than a night or two they both needed to replenish their wardrobes.

Although she had several changes of clothes in the closet, for some reason she no longer wished to appear in dowdy gowns when she had a wardrobe full of outfits at Draycot Manor that showed her at her best. She glanced down, smiling ruefully at the generous bosom the good Lord had seen fit to bestow on her. If only the rest of her frame matched this excess of femininity. Unfortunately, apart from her breasts, she was slender almost to the point of thinness. Her waist was tiny, but then so were her hips and she had no roundness at the rear at all.

She grinned, thanking God that at least from the front no one could mistake her for a boy. She leant across to pick up the glass of boiled water from the side-table by her bed wincing as her hair, trapped behind her shoulders, tugged her scalp. The sudden pain made her angry again. She hated being an invalid, and lolling around in bed was not something she enjoyed. She wanted to be up about and solving the mystery of Aunt Agatha's disappearance.

She heard the door opening in the sitting-room adjacent to her bedchamber and, assuming it was Birdie, called out cheerfully, 'Come straight in, I'm feeling much better, and believe I could eat a bowl of soup if any is to be found.'

The door swung wide, but instead of her companion she found herself staring at a man whose bulk entirely blocked the doorway. Hester swallowed nervously – she'd no idea her adversary was a giant.

'I'm afraid I've brought no soup, Miss Frobisher, but I do have some humble pie, and news about Aunt Agatha, if you will allow me to come in.'

Forgetting the fact that she was sitting in her nightgown, her hair floating in russet waves around her shoulders and that she was about to allow her cousin to breach convention in the most disastrous of ways, she agreed. There were a few things she wished to say to this man. She addressed him sweetly.

'Please, *do* come in, my lord; I have been wishing to speak to you this age.'

She saw him look around for somewhere to sit and seeing a plain wooden chair, strolled across to collect it. She watched with interest as he placed it as far away from the bed as he could without actually being in the next room. It was only then she understood she should never have invited him in. Too late to repine: he was here, and he wasn't leaving until she'd received some answers.

'Miss Bird, my companion, will be back at any moment, so I'm sure if you remain in the open doorway, no one can consider we have breached convention.'

She saw his mouth twitch, and he raised an eyebrow. She felt herself colour under his scrutiny and her pithy words deserted her. Why did this man seem so familiar? He was a stranger, could she have met him before?

Then she realized. Her hand came up to touch a strand of her own hair; his was the exact same shade, and it waved a little as it fell across his brow as hers did. His eyes were also hazel, and he had the same thick black lashes rimming them. They came from different branches of the family, but by some quirk of fate had inherited a similar colouring.

'I know, Miss Frobisher. We're only distantly related, but some oddity of nature has made us seem like siblings.' He smiled, and her heart jumped unexpectedly in her chest. She felt something flicker down her spine. 'However, there the similarity ends. I think I could be compared to a farm horse whilst you, my dear cousin, are a thoroughbred.'

A thoroughbred? Comparing a lady to a horse, however well bred, was unacceptable. Her eyes glittered dangerously. 'I believe that was meant to be a compliment, sir; however, I don't consider that being compared to an equine is something a young lady aspires to.' She studied him closely; he was surely the broadest man she'd ever set eyes on. He must have made a formidable soldier.

'I beg your pardon, Miss Frobisher, it was not my intention to offend.' His words were conciliatory, but his eyes remained watchful.

She lowered her lids, attempting to marshal her wandering thoughts. She found it oddly disturbing having such a man in the same room. She heard a slight scrape of a chair and knew he'd moved, knew he was standing closer.

'Are you well, Miss Frobisher? Shall I fetch Miss Bird?'

She opened her eyes. This was the opportunity she had been waiting for. 'I'm remarkably well, Colebrook, considering you attempted to murder me a few days ago.'

He stiffened and his nostrils pinched. 'I have come to apologize for that grievous error, Miss Frobisher.'

She cut him short. 'Do not. What you did was inexcusable. Even if I had been an intruder such gratuitous violence was quite unnecessary.'

He moved back to stand behind the chair, his expression closed. 'I am a professional soldier, I make no apologies for that. I heard a noise. How was I to know it was you who were skulking around upstairs like a burglar?'

A burglar? How dare he refer to her as such? She had as much right to be at Neddingfield as he. 'You're not a soldier, sir, you're a peer of the realm and should behave as befits your station. Such violent behaviour is quite unacceptable amongst the aristocracy, you know.'

She tensed, waiting for his reply. She did not expect it to be a polite one. Instead he laughed and resumed his seat. 'I have no wish to bandy insults with you, miss. I do not deliberately mistreat members of the fair sex.' He smiled. His teeth flashed white and for a second time her heart behaved most erratically. Hester found her anger melting beneath his charm.

'It's a little late to remember that, my lord.' She returned his smile reluctantly. 'I think, then, that I shall consider myself David to your Goliath.'

This comment flummoxed him. His eyes narrowed as he tried to decide exactly what she meant. She hoped he'd come to the conclusion she intended; that he might be three times her weight, but she would defeat him by her intelligence.

He leant forward, his eyes glittering strangely. 'I do believe, my dear, that you're throwing down a challenge. Do you think we are to be adversaries?'

'Sir, I believe I'm correct when I say that you attacked me viciously. I'm lucky to have escaped with something as slight as a concussion.'

'I came here, Miss Frobisher, to offer my most humble and sincere apologies for injuring you. I have no excuse—'

'Then pray don't offer one, your apology is now accepted.' For a moment she thought she'd gone too far, that her flippancy had angered him. She saw his jaw harden, and braced herself for a set down. To her astonishment his chuckles filled the room.

'My God, you're an original! It's refreshing to meet someone who has the temerity to stand up to me.'

'In which case, as I have accepted *your* apology, are you ready to answer *my* questions?'

He sobered. 'Of course. I'm sure there are many things you would like to know, not least why plain Mr Sinclair is now dancing around like a popinjay calling himself the Earl of Waverly – Colebrook to his friends, of course.' He said this with a decided sneer.

Hester viewed him uncertainly. Was he jesting? He sounded as disgusted as she that he had inherited a title. Surely he didn't share her radical views? 'Yes, that is one of the things I'd like to know. You don't seem overly pleased to be so honoured.'

'I'm a plain man. I told you, I've been a professional soldier all my life, with neither the desire nor the appropriate training to take a place in high society. But it seems there was a connection that led the legal crows to me. So here I am, no longer Major Sinclair, but Lord Colebrook.'

Hester was beginning to enjoy this conversation, she was feeling more alive and stimulated than she had for months. She heard footsteps approaching across the sitting-room. She frowned, knowing they were both in disgrace.

'My lord, you are *de trop*. Miss Frobisher is not receiving. Kindly remove yourself at once.'

She watched her cousin leap to his feet and bow deeply to her outraged companion. He didn't glance her way and, without uttering a further word, vanished from the room leaving her feeling sadly flat.

'My dear, whatever were you thinking? Colebrook should not be in here; you're scarcely decent. You should have sent him packing, and he should have had more sense than to stay.'

'Please don't be cross, Birdie. He's my cousin after all, and although we're only distantly connected, did you see how alike we are? He could be my brother, couldn't he?'

Birdie snorted inelegantly. 'That's as maybe, miss, but he isn't your brother, and has no right to take liberties as though he was. Now, I have excellent news for you. A girl has been found whom

Tom thinks will make an ideal abigail for you, a Polly Makepeace. He says she's quietly spoken and intelligent. When she arrives, if I agree with his assessment, I shall appoint her. Tom said that he passed her on the lane some time ago, so I can't think what's keeping her.'

Hester was delighted, if she had a maid to attend her she could sit in the parlour and entertain her cousin, and would be suitably chaperoned even when Birdie was busy elsewhere.

'That's good news. Because you sent my cousin away I have yet to discover what he knows about Aunt Agatha. I don't suppose you heard what it was?'

'No, I'm afraid I didn't. However, Bill is about to return to Draycot with our carriage; he thinks he will be home by mid-afternoon and can return with Jane, and what we require, tomorrow morning.'

'That's excellent, Birdie. When you were in the study, did you find any clues as to why my aunt should have disappeared so suddenly?'

Birdie shook her head. 'Of course I didn't, my dear. I was hardly going to poke about amongst things that are no concern of mine. It's barely acceptable for you and Lord Colebrook to examine Miss Culley's private papers, but it would be outside of enough for someone like me to touch them.'

Hester changed the subject. 'This girl, how is it that she's available at such short notice?'

'It's very odd; it appears that her mistress collapsed and died on the way back from market yesterday. The girl was working locally, you know, and Tom says gossip in the town seems to point to what's going on up here as being to blame for the poor lady's death.'

'I hardly see how that could be the cause of this lady's fatal apoplexy.' Hester shuddered, the longer she was here the more she felt that something sinister was waiting to announce itself.

She thought that it must be her injury making her fanciful. After all she was renowned for her common sense.

'Perhaps the lady was of a volatile nature, and the thought of what happened frightened her to death.' It seemed highly unlikely that such a thing could happen, but others were less pragmatic than she.

'There's murmuring about witchcraft and ghosts. Maybe the girl felt she had no choice but to leave her employment before she found herself accused of being responsible for her mistress's untimely end.'

The sound of movement in the dressing-room made Hester pause. 'I think that might be her, Birdie. Call her in at once; if she's a local girl, she might well be able to help me with my investigations.'

She watched her friend cross the room, her footsteps silent on the carpet. She could tell from her rigid stance that she disapproved of any reference to investigations. She could hear her talking to someone in the dressing-room. She felt perfectly well and was intending to ask this new maid, Polly, to help her get dressed as soon as Birdie went off again to organize matters downstairs.

She couldn't see the dressing-room from the bed and her head was still too sore to risk turning, so she would have to contain her impatience until the girl appeared.

'My dear, that wasn't Polly, it was Meg bringing you up some hot water. There's concern downstairs that something untoward might have happened to the other girl. It would seem that when the rest of the new staff walked up the drive earlier they saw no sign of her.'

'But didn't you say Tom passed her on the road?'

'He did. He's going out with his lordship and his man to scour the grounds. There's a short cut through the wood and they think that's the way she must have come. Don't look so worried, my dear. I expect the girl's twisted her ankle and is sitting at the side of the path as we speak waiting for someone to rescue her.'

'Where's Jet? He should go with them. If Polly's lost or hurt he'll find her. Go down and tell Tom to take him.' Hester knew she shouldn't order her dear friend in such a way, but for some reason she believed the girl's life might depend on her hound being included in the search.

Chapter Six

RALPH WAITED OUTSIDE in the turning circle for his makeshift army to ready itself. He was astride Thunder and Clark and James were mounted. It was Robin and the foot soldiers who were not yet ready. He had selected the four fittest of the roughly dressed men who had come from town and issued them with stout cudgels.

He spotted the arrival of Miss Bird in the mêlée and guided his mount towards her, leaning down from his saddle in order to speak to her.

'Miss Bird, is something wrong? Can I be assistance?'

'My lord, Miss Frobisher suggests that you take her hound, Jet, with you. If this young girl is injured or lost in the woods he's the one to find her.'

'Excellent notion, ma'am. I made the acquaintance of the animal yesterday but didn't realize he belonged to Miss Frobisher.' He straightened, turning to shout across to Robin, who had just emerged from the stable block leading his mount. 'Robin, find that dog. Miss Bird suggests we take him with us. He was around here earlier.'

Tom overheard and shouted Jet's name and the massive animal appeared at his side, tongue lolling, head to one side, waiting for instructions. Ralph was beginning to warm to the animal. He glanced at his group and nodded; they weren't many, but they were sufficient to scare off any intruders in the wood. He raised his arm and led the group towards the rear of the house, to the path that led directly to the gates. When he'd questioned the other new arrivals it had confirmed his fears.

This girl should have arrived at the Hall over an hour ago. He hoped she had merely suffered a mishap and was sitting crying on the pathway waiting to be found. If she had hurt herself, surely those who had walked past on the drive would have heard her shouting?

'Tom, you lead with the dog. I'll follow directly behind with Robin; we're both armed and can protect your back if needs be.'

'Very well, my lord. Jet will hear anything long before we do. If the lass is in the wood, this fellow will lead us to her.'

Ralph knew he really meant, if the girl was still living. For God's sake! Why should they all be imagining the worst? It was damned unsettling to be in the middle of something dangerous and not know who his enemy was.

They cantered into the wood, the men on foot jogging behind. Soon they were forced to slow and progress single file. He listened, but could hear no sound of crying. The wood was too quiet, the birds had fallen silent too.

'Tom, send the dog off. We'll dismount and lead the horses.' He watched the massive animal lope off, nose to the ground. The path widened slightly and he stooped to examine a slight disturbance.

'I've found footprints here, at least two sets; they stopped, then returned at speed. I don't like the look of this, Robin, these are fresh and made by boots, well-repaired ones at that.'

He reached into his belt and withdrew his pistol, holding the reins in one hand, his pistol in the other he walked forward. They moved quietly, only the occasional clink of a bit or the snort of a horse audible in the gloom. He raised his pistol indicating that the men behind him halt. He tethered his horse, intending to continue without the hindrance of their mounts.

He heard the others do the same. Half crouching in the shadows cast by the overhanging branches, he led them on. Ralph was certain they were not alone in the woods, somewhere just ahead, evil stalked.

They all heard the screams. Ralph broke into a run. The girl must be in fear for her life. Tom, who was in front of him, veered off the path, crashing through the undergrowth, taking the direct route, using the shrieks to guide him.

Tom shouted back. 'The dog's ahead; like a bullet he was. He'll be there before us and if he doesn't stop the bastards, nothing will.'

Ralph didn't answer, using his breath to fuel his feet. He could hear the others close behind, and prayed they would not be too late. Suddenly the air was torn by a bloodcurdling roar, followed by a second scream this time of agony, not fear. From that moment it was impossible to distinguish the growls and snarls of the dog from the screams of the man he was savaging.

Cocking his pistol, he pushed his sleeves back leaving his hands free. With a final surge he burst into a scene resembling a gladiatorial arena. There was only one man lying under a holly tree, the dog crouched over him, jaws dripping, throat rumbling in a steady snarl. There was no sign of the girl; she was no longer screaming and he feared she had been taken by the other assailant.

A faint cry in the branches above his head alerted him. Balanced precariously, at the top of the tree was a grey shape; he could just distinguish a pale face staring down at him.

'Polly? You're safe now, sweetheart. I'll be up to fetch you soon; hold on a while longer. There are things to be sorted out down here.'

He looked at the gruesome mess that had once been the face of a man. He didn't want the girl to see this, not after everything else she had endured. He spoke sharply to Jet. 'Enough, Jet, leave.'

To the amazement of those standing rigid around the body, the dog relaxed, wagging his tail, backing away from the cadaver as his long pink tongue cleaned his bloodstained jowls. The animal padded over to push his head against Ralph's leg seeking approval. Ralph reached down and pulled one of the silky ears.

'Good dog, you've done well. Perhaps a little too well.'

He'd seen too many bodies during his life as a soldier to find this one particularly upsetting. His only regret was that the man had died before he could be asked why he was trying to kidnap a servant girl.

'Robin, get this object out of sight, empty the pockets then get one of the men to bury it somewhere in the woods.'

'Yes, my lord. What about the other one? Do you want us to go after him?'

'Yes; take two men with you and the dog. He can't have got far. Jet will soon find him.'

He tossed his pistol to James, removed his riding cape and then shrugged out of his topcoat. He felt the cold of the wind through his cotton shirt sleeves. The girl must be freezing up there. 'I'm going to fetch her down. One of you bring the horses; she'll be unable to walk back. She must have been cowering up there for over an hour.'

'Shall I go up for you, my lord? I'm used to climbing trees.'

'Thank you, James, I shall finish the job myself.' His long arms had no difficulty finding a grip and within moments he was beside the shivering girl. 'Don't try and talk; you can tell me what happened later.' The girl, scarcely more than a child really, nodded, and attempted a smile.

He braced himself, then nodded reassuringly. 'Place your arms round my neck, sweetheart, and I'll take you down as easy as winking.' He saw her doubt and knew she was too scared to move of her own volition.

'Look at the size of me. I could carry three of you dangling from my neck and still climb up and down this tree with no difficulty. I don't know about you, but I'm in need of some refreshment after all this activity.' As he was speaking he gently prised the girl's fingers away from the branch and pulled her close until her legs were dangling around his waist and her arms securely locked about his neck.

'Make the most of this, Polly, you'll not get carried in the arms of an aristocrat many times more in your life.' He felt her relax into him, and slipped his left arm about her waist. 'Right, here we go.'

It was not quite as easy as he'd pretended, and he was obliged to take the full weight of himself and his burden on one outstretched arm on two occasions before he eventually reached the lower branches. Then willing hands reached up to remove the girl and he jumped the last six feet. His boots squelched unpleasantly in the reddened dirt under the tree. James appeared with the horses.

'Here, hand me my things. Once I'm dressed, we can get back.'

The girl, cradled in Tom's arms, spoke for the first time. 'Excuse me, sir, it was my bag falling from the tree that alerted the men and it has all my belongings in it. Is it still here, or has the other one taken it away with him?'

'I'll get the men to look for it; don't worry about it now. If it's lost, then I'll see that everything is replaced for you. It's more important to get you out of the cold.'

He didn't offer to take her up in front of him, leaving it to Tom, who seemed quite content to keep the plucky girl in his care. He left the mundane tasks to others. Without waiting for Robin's return with the second man, he mounted and set off. When Polly recovered would be soon enough to ask questions. He shivered. It was damn cold, cold enough for snow.

*

The man in the doorway, clutching his cap, was visibly shaking. Bertram had no time for such weakness. 'So, not only did you fail to bring that girl back as instructed, your partner has been mauled to death by a wolf. I'm waiting for an explanation, damn you. Am I surrounded by incompetents? I set you both a simple task, to bring back a maidservant called Polly Makepeace, and you can't even do that.'

He turned his back on his minion and heard the man shuffle backwards into the icy hall and back presumably to the warmth of the kitchen. Bertram unclenched his fists and breathed in deeply, trying to control his rage. One of his retainers told him he had overheard the under groom saying he had a sweetheart living in Little Neddingfield and he'd been desperate to get hold of the girl ever since.

He'd done his planning so meticulously; knew that Miss Culley went abroad frequently and took her staff with her. The only two who remained behind were the elderly housekeeper and cook who were dispatched to stay in a small house in Bath that Miss Culley owned.

His lips curved in the pretence of a smile. The old ladies had been dispatched all right, but not to the same place as expected. They were both so old; it had been more than time for them to stop cluttering up the world with their presence.

But the girl had now slipped through his fingers and he needed to be sure she wouldn't blab to the major about Miss Culley's connection to France. He wanted this man to believe that the rumours were true and that it was the supernatural that had spirited away his relative and all her retainers.

He stared out of the window watching the trees moving restlessly in the icy wind. The idiot who was acting as cook had said it was likely to snow: so much the better, the major would be trapped and unable to send out for reinforcements. He had spent his remaining funds on renting this old house and employing a dozen and a half ex-soldiers, those not too fussy how they earned their pay.

A slight prickle of unease flickered through him. When he'd decided there would be ghosts at Neddingfield Hall, and had initiated the talk about strange sightings and disappearances, only he had known it to be false. His men were able to vanish at will into the underground cellar his father had described to him, leaving no evidence of their passage behind them. But the man who had just returned after his failed attempt to capture the one weak link in his scheme, had been terrified, convinced that the very hound of Hell had emerged from nowhere to kill his partner in the most frightful way.

He shrugged; no matter, if his men were frightened so much the better: scared men fought harder in his experience. It would add credence to his story that the Hall was haunted and the local villagers wouldn't dare venture into the woods to see what was happening. The major was going to lose all his new staff very soon as well.

Demonic laughter echoed around the shabby room and the rough man outside the door flinched away and scurried back to his snug billet in the bowels of the house; the message he carried was never delivered.

Hester insisted on getting dressed after washing. The physician had advised she stay in bed for three days, but hadn't said it was essential. 'The Hall sounds more like it should now that there are people moving around and the fires are lit and candles every-where.'

'Well, my dear, I did not come here expecting to take on the role of housekeeper, but there's no one else to do the job so I hope you'll excuse me if I cannot be with you all the time.'

'Birdie, you must do whatever's necessary to ensure the smooth running of the household. I'm thankful Tom managed to find a cook; what was served this morning was all but inedible.'

Her friend chuckled. 'I've been assured that there will be fresh vegetable soup, newly baked bread, and apple pie and cheese ready soon. Now, my dear, if you're comfortably settled here in front of the fire I shall take my leave. Meg's in your chamber, ring that handbell beside you and she'll come to assist you.'

Hester smiled; as long as she got her lunch when it was ready there was nothing else she required. Her head ached, her eyes were a trifle blurred so she would stretch out in front of the log fire and try and think of a reason for what was happening. She was dozing comfortably when she heard heavy footsteps approaching her parlour.

She swung her feet to the floor, removing her lap-rug and checking that her hair was still tied tidily at the back of her neck. Her head was too sore to put it up in its usual arrangement. She reached out and rang the bell. If his lordship was coming to visit she would not make the same mistake: this time she would be chaperoned. The knock on the door sounded as the maid appeared from the bedchamber.

'See who that is, please, Meg. If it is Lord Colebrook, bid him enter.'

The girl dipped in a brief curtsy, smoothed her apron and hurried to open the door. Hester smiled as he stepped round the girl and walked in without a by your leave.

'You're looking much better today, Miss Frobisher. As you're fully dressed, and we're not alone, I shall assume it's acceptable for me to stay.'

'Of course it is, my lord. You're very welcome. Tell me, is Polly safely back with you?'

'She is. I have already spoken to her and she's fully recovered. We have your hound to thank for her deliverance.'

By the time he had told her the whole, Hester wasn't sure if she was pleased or horrified.

'Good gracious! I never knew he could be so ... so ferocious. I've not had him all that long, you see. He was a stray. I found him with his paw caught in a trap and nursed him well. Since then he's been my constant companion.' She saw his brow crease and knew that for some reason this information did not please him.

'That dog is not a pet; he's a hunting dog. I think it better if I keep him.'

She almost choked. 'Keep him? You certainly shall not, sir. He's my dog, and the fact that he killed a man today is neither here nor there. He would never harm me, and he was only doing his duty.' She glared at him. How dare he march into her apartment and start issuing ultimatums in this way? 'Another thing, I don't remember giving you leave to ride my horse either.'

He leant back in the deep-seated armchair crossing his long legs at the ankle and folding his arms across his chest before deigning to answer. He stared at her, and she pressed herself into the seat. 'It might have escaped your attention, my girl, that you are a female and I am quite definitely the head of your household. I'm your only male relative and as such it is my prerogative to borrow your horse and your dog whenever I see fit to do so.'

Hester was speechless. The more she saw of this person the more she disliked him. She shook her head as if to rid herself of his presence. The sudden movement sent a violent jolt of pain through her and she flinched, closing her eyes to allow it to subside.

'You are in pain. I am a brute to bark at you when you're still an invalid.'

She was aware that he had left his seat for she could feel the heat from his body and smell a distinctive aroma of lavender soap and leather wafting into her nostrils. She hardly dare open her eyes, not sure what she would be faced with. Staring back at her were a pair of identical hazel eyes. He was too close. Such proximity made her nervous and her heart race.

'I moved my head too fast, my lord. I'm quite well now, thank you.' She hoped he'd take the hint that she wished him to remove himself back to his chair on the other side of the grate.

He didn't move. Instead, she saw him slowly raise his right hand and knew he was going to touch her. She flinched away. Instantly he was on his feet, his expression polite, no sign of that disturbing glitter in his eyes.

'I shall not keep you much longer, Miss Frobisher, but I wished to tell you what I have discovered so far. Shall I return tomorrow when you're feeling more the thing?'

'I told you, I'm feeling perfectly well. We haven't yet settled the nonsensical matter of *you* believing you are my guardian.'

He raised an eyebrow and relaxed, hooking his arm around the back of the chair in an infuriating manner. 'That isn't open for discussion, my dear girl. It's a fact. Indisputable. Whilst we're both here I am morally and legally responsible for you.'

She bit her lip. He was right; women, even those who'd reached their majority, were so regarded by the law. Perhaps whilst she was incarcerated at Neddingfield she should pretend to accept his authority and in that way she would at least be able to participate in the solving of this mystery.

'Very well; you have my permission to ride Thunder and take care of Jet.'

'Thank you. Have I also your permission to—'

'If we are not to be at daggers drawn, my lord, I would much prefer it if you desisted from poking fun at me.' She gave him no time to answer, merely smiled brightly and ploughed on, 'I've been thinking of nothing else but what has taken place here. I believe I might have come up with something. However, before

I expound my theories I would like to hear the facts you have, for they might contradict my deductions.'

'I shall tell you all I know, which, I warn you, is not much. I'm certain that both Aunt Agatha and the staff left here on horse-back the day before we arrived. I'm also certain that they went willingly, and may have been duped by a band of men masquerading as soldiers. I can also tell you that Polly, the girl who was almost abducted today, believed they were looking for her particularly. She told me she's walking out with the under-groom – you would have known him, Sam Roberts?' Hester nodded and regretted it. 'This is the girl's only connection to Neddingfield. Whoever is behind this needs Sam Roberts's betrothed.'

Neither spoke for a moment, both mulling over the facts. The crackling of the logs and the wind rattling the shutters was the only sound in the room.

'What you've told me, Lord Colebrook, more or less fits in with what I had surmised. You have found no sign of anyone within a few miles of here, which makes me think they must have boarded a ship.' She waited for him to laugh at her expla-nation but he didn't: he spoke on another subject entirely.

'Do you know, I'm heartily sick of being called *Lord Colebrook* and *my lord* by all and sundry. We are related – could you not bring yourself to call me by my given name?'

'Call you *Ralph*? I should think not; we're barely acquainted. Miss Bird would fly up in the boughs at such a thing.' Her lips twitched, unable to resist his pleading look. 'I shall call you Cousin Ralph; that must be acceptable.'

'Thank you. I shall address you in future as Cousin Hester. Now, that's settled, let me think about your theory.' He slapped his thigh, the sudden sound startling her. 'Good Lord! I think you're right. We haven't found them, and they were certainly heading towards the coast. However, that doesn't explain what persuaded Aunt Agatha to leave in the dead of night to embark on a sea journey in November.'

'What about the horses? Surely they wouldn't have taken them? I know Thunder hates to walk across a bridge, let alone board a ship. If they left by sea, we should find their mounts hidden near the coast. Have your men looked for them?'

His eyes widened. 'Looked for the horses? One looks very like another, unless you've seen them before. Could you pick out any of Aunt Agatha's livestock from a field of similar beasts?'

'No, I suppose not. But the four greys that pulled her coach, they must be easily distinguished. Send men out right away to search. Forget about the people, find the animals and we'll be halfway there.'

She saw his amusement fade and realized she had offended him with her orders. Too late, she understood he was not a man to be told what to do in such a peremptory fashion. Should she apologize or wait until he'd given her a set down? She didn't have to wait long.

He began pleasantly enough, his tone bland, leaning forward slightly as if to emphasize his point. 'Pray forgive me if I have misunderstood, Miss Frobisher. You're suggesting I send my men out now? In the dark?'

Hester didn't answer. She felt it might be a rhetorical question so decided to say nothing. This was her second error.

'I asked you a question, miss, and I expect an answer.'

He spoke to her as though she was a child. It was enough to give her the courage to speak. 'My lord, I most humbly beg your pardon for daring to voice my opinions to someone as toplofty as yourself. I am, as you reminded me so kindly, a female and as such cannot be expected to have anything worth saying.'

She stood up, swaying slightly at the effort, and waited for him to do the same. She curtsied, intending it to be a gesture of contempt, to demonstrate how little she thought of his elevation to the aristocracy or his highhanded manners. As she lowered her head a wave of dizziness swept over her and to her horror she tumbled forward and was unable to do anything to prevent it.

'Idiot girl!'

She felt herself being lifted and held, as if she belonged there, close to his heart. Instinctively she relaxed, he might be an arrogant brute, but he was more than capable of holding her safely. She could hear Meg fluttering about in the background obviously unsure what her role was.

'Put me back on the *chaise-longue*, if you please, my lord.' She felt his chest vibrate under her cheek and knew he was laughing at her. 'Please, Cousin Ralph, I should like you to put me down.'

This time he responded and gently lowered her back to the day-bed. He stepped away, leaving Meg to hurry forward to fuss with her pillows and the comforter she had discarded earlier. By the time the girl had finished he was gone.

'Enough, Meg. Please fetch me a glass of lemonade; then go downstairs and find out from Miss Bird when Polly will be well enough to take up her duties.'

The girl left silently and Hester knew that yet again she had spoken without thought. Her desire to be left alone had made her forget that her words could be construed as a criticism of the service she had been receiving. Sighing, disappointed with herself, she closed her eyes vowing to do better next time, especially in her dealings with Lord Colebrook.

Chapter Seven

HESTER WOKE WITHOUT a headache and the lump on the side of her head had almost disappeared. She was determined today she would go downstairs to meet the rest of the staff. Jet and Thunder must also think she had abandoned them, for this was the longest time she'd spent apart from her two companions. She frowned; they were not, according to her cousin, her responsibility any longer.

She sat up in bed and was immediately struck by an eerie silence. It was still early, she could see from the mantel clock it was just after seven and it would be quite dark outside, but it was more than that: there was a total absence of noise.

Snow! It must have fallen overnight. Without pausing to push her feet into her slippers, or her arms into her robe, she ran across to the window. The heavy curtains rattled noisily as she pulled them apart.

'Oh, Miss Frobisher, that's not your job. I was just on my way in with your chocolate. Why don't you get back into bed, and let me do it for you?'

Hester found herself gently escorted back to bed by a girl who looked no more than sixteen, her mouse-brown hair neatly pulled into a knot and covered with a white cap. This must be Polly Makepeace.

'Polly, I'm so pleased to see you. Are you fully recovered from your misadventure?'

A shadow slid across the girl's face but then she pinned on a smile 'I'm right as rain, miss. Sitting up a tree for an hour or so did me no harm. I'm that sorry I caused so much bother.' The blankets were back across her knees and the pillows plumped behind before Hester could protest. 'There. You might be feeling better, miss, but it's not right you should draw the curtains yourself. That's what I'm paid for.'

'I wanted to see if it had snowed overnight. It's so quiet.'

'It has, at least three inches of the horrible stuff. It might look pretty, but I can tell you it's no fun for those who have to work outside.'

Hester smiled. She knew she was going to deal well with this girl. She spoke her mind, like she did, and would make an ideal abigail until Jane arrived. 'Goodness! If there's been so much snow my carriage won't arrive, neither will my maid.'

'In that case, it's a good thing I'm here to look after you.'

'I don't suppose one of your many skills includes sewing?'

'It does, Miss Frobisher. I altered all Mrs Mills's gowns for her. She lost a lot of weight last year, after she was ill.' She saw the girl swallow and turn away. It was sad that someone so young should have endured so much.

'In that case, Polly, come and have a look at the garments hanging in my closet. If I showed you some fashion plates from *La Belle Assemblée* do you think you could adapt any of them to match? If I'm not to have my new gowns, then maybe you can resurrect my old ones. The material is good, it's just the cut that's a trifle out-dated.'

She smoothed down the velveteen skirt of the solitary day dress she had brought with her.

'You'll notice I have no pastels or white amongst my clothes; I wear colours that suit me, not what convention dictates.'

The two were standing in front of the huge wardrobe. Polly picked out an evening gown, the waist fashionably high, but the skirt plain, no ruffles or rouleau, and none of the fullness that typified current modes. The girl ran the russet silk between her fingers, smiling in appreciation.

'This one's lovely, miss. I can use the train to inset two pieces in the skirt and make it wider. The bodice and sleeves are perfect.'

'Please begin at once. I shall keep Meg as well, then you can devote most of your time to sewing.'

The matter settled satisfactorily, she turned away, pleased that fate had brought Polly to her. Whatever happened, she would try and persuade the girl to stay. She loved Jane, but she lacked the sharp wits she had detected in her new maid.

Downstairs she was happy to find things much more as she was used to. The wide corridors were still cold and draughty, but this was normal, for Aunt Agatha never had fires lit anywhere but the main reception rooms and bedchambers. She was delighted to discover a large fire burning in the grate of the grand entrance hall; it seemed two trees had been dragged in and set ablaze. It made a pleasant change to be able to walk across the vast space without one's breath freezing.

Although the place was tidy and the fires burning, she had, so far, met none of the new staff. Birdie had said there were over a dozen inside staff appointed and half-a-dozen men out. Where was everyone?

She glanced out of the window and saw the snow had blown into substantial drifts across the drive. It looked beautiful, like something from a fairytale, but no coaches would be on the road today, that's for sure. She decided to go to the breakfast parlour, hoping the new cook had provided hot food, as she, as always, was famished.

The room showed signs of recent occupation. His lordship had obviously already eaten and departed. Not sure if she was relieved or disappointed, Hester tugged the bell-strap and while waiting for attention, lifted the silver lids to see what delicacies had been provided for them this morning.

There were crisp slices of ham, coddled eggs, fresh bread and preserves. More than enough to make a substantial breakfast. She piled her plate and took it to the table, deciding to sit with her back to the fire; from here she could watch the door and see across the park. She was halfway through her repast when the door opened and her companion hurried in.

'What are you doing up, my dear? I'm sure I remember Dr Radcliff saying you must remain in your rooms for another day at least.'

'As you can see, Birdie, I'm fully recovered and refuse to remain upstairs any longer. Where is Lord Colebrook, do you know?'

She waited whilst Birdie filled her own plate and brought it over to sit next to her. 'He's out with some of the men. They're riding down to the coast; it seems they believe your aunt might have been spirited away on a boat. I wonder what gave them that crackbrained notion?'

'It was I. It's the only possible explanation. A large ship can anchor easily in the bay and rowing boats come ashore to collect passengers. Aunt Agatha has arrived and departed that way several times; though I have no idea why she should have been persuaded to do this when she had just invited us to visit.'

'I hope you're not intending to meddle in affairs that are best left to Lord Colebrook, my dear.'

Hester knew better than to tell Birdie she was determined to be involved, and already her cousin had taken his men out into the snow in order to follow her instructions.

'It's a good thing we're snug and well provided for here. I doubt if anyone will be able to visit, or bring us extra provisions until the snow has gone.'

'It's unseasonably early to be so cold. I'm sure it will not last long; it rarely does when it comes before Christmastide. I found Polly sitting in your bedchamber altering an evening gown for you. Are you intending to dress for dinner?'

Hester flushed; this was exactly what she wished to do. She wanted to show her cousin that she was not a child, but a young woman of equal standing. By so doing, if she was honest, she would also appear at her best. This was a new experience for her; she had always dressed to please herself, but for some reason she wanted Colebrook to know she was as sophisticated and elegant as anyone he might meet as a peer of the realm.

'I have to wear something in the evening. Good heavens, surely you do not intend to sit down to dine with Colebrook dressed any old how?'

'I do not intend to dine with him at all, my dear. It's not my place to sit with you and Lord Colebrook. I'm the housekeeper at the moment, and although I intend to eat breakfast and luncheon with you – in the evening I shall have a tray in my room as befits my station.'

Hester stared suspiciously. Since when had Birdie worried about such matters? They did everything together, when she entertained friends at either the town house or at Draycot Manor, her companion always sat at table with them. 'That's nonsense, and you know it. You always eat with Aunt Agatha and me. Why should anything be different just because my cousin has been elevated?'

'Things *are* different, my dear, because I am assuming the role of housekeeper and in order to do this properly, I cannot have a foot in both camps so to speak. It's perfectly acceptable to dine alone with someone who's related to you. I believe his lordship explained that you're in his charge now. Although you're of age, and have full control of your fortune, whilst we're here, I'm afraid, you'll have to accept that he's standing as your guardian.'

So that was how the land lay. Hester's first suspicions about her summons to Neddingfield Hall were not so far out after all. Where Aunt Agatha had left off, her companion was continuing. It was patent nonsense that she was in any way under the control of her cousin, but if it pleased them both to believe she accepted this, then so be it. She knew it was Birdie's intention to throw the two of them together and hope that they might suit.

'Very well, it will do no good to argue, I can see that your mind's made up on the matter. However, I'm adamant that I shall dress appropriately when I *do* decide to come down to dine. You can be sure that his lordship will not appear in his riding boots and topcoat. Haven't you noticed, for all he says he's a plain man, his clothes are made by Weston, and his shirts are of the finest lawn.'

She stopped, flustered, knowing she had revealed far too much and wasn't surprised that her friend smiled, resuming her breakfast with renewed relish.

The sun glittered on the snow making it hard to see any distance without being dazzled. Ralph reined in, standing in his stirrups in order to see over the hedge that boarded the lane.

'Look, that farm over there, it has several large barns – the horses could be hidden inside there. There's smoke coming from the chimney stack, so someone's in residence.'

'It's the first place we've come to that looks a possibility, my lord. That last village we passed was deserted – and the other man vanished into thin air yesterday, just like all the others.'

Ralph didn't wish to be reminded; they had rescued the girl and that had to be enough. 'Forget about it, Robin. Consider – we're within a mile of the coast. What would the sound of horses mean to these folk?' When his man looked puzzled, he chuckled. 'Customs officers, that's who they thought we were. This is smugglers' territory; they must go in permanent fear of being raided by the excise men. I don't doubt that all the men in this village are eking out their miserable existence by being involved in some way in illegal trading. They'll not have seen or heard anything; they've learnt to look the other way.'

The farm showed signs of earlier activity. There were footprints, black in the snow, leading to the privy at the rear and also further tracks to one of the larger buildings. Ralph kicked his feet from the stirrups, dropping to the ground, glad *his* boots were watertight.

'Robin, take James and go and search the barns whilst I speak to the occupants of this hovel.'

They both carried a pair of pistols, primed and ready. He felt more comfortable knowing there were fully armed men behind him.

He waited whilst Tom tethered both horses to a convenient rail and then strode to the door and hammered on it. There was no response. He thumped again. This time he heard sounds of shuffling feet in the passageway. The door opened slowly and a wizened face peered round.

'You come for them dratted 'orses at last? They been 'ere long enough. I ain't going out in this weather to feed 'em again, that's for sure. I weren't paid enough to do for them when it's bitter.' The hunched old man nodded to emphasize his words and then slammed the door in Ralph's face.

Nonplussed, he stared at the peeling wood, not sure if he was outraged or amused. He heard a smothered laugh and swung round.

'Well, Tom, at least we know we've come to the right place. Whoever arranged for the horses to be stabled here, obviously didn't intend for them to be here so long.'

'I'm not sure, my lord; isn't it possible they don't care if the horses are discovered? This is the first place anyone would look.'

'No, I think the bad weather has delayed them. Whoever left

them here intends to return for them at some point. I'm certain we were not expected to find them so quickly. The old man was probably not paid for more than a few days.'

He walked, almost knee deep in places, through the snow and found the other two in the barn examining the missing beasts, which looked cold and miserable in their unaccustomed squalor.

Robin greeted him cheerfully. 'I recognize the greys, sir; these are definitely the animals Miss Culley uses to pull her carriage. They've not been looked after. James is searching for some rope, I think we can lead them back, if we take three each. I reckon, Tom, you'll have to go back into town and find some more men to act as grooms.'

The horses were led out. The first of each trio had a second lead rein attached to their halter allowing each man to lead his small group. Ralph prayed they could get the horses, and themselves, back without mishap.

He wondered if he should leave someone here to see who came back to collect the animals, but decided against it. He was seriously short of manpower and every instinct told him this was only the beginning. The man orchestrating these events had intended he should be unnerved, that he would think the strange disappearance witchcraft, or some other such fustian, but he had now disproved that theory. What he didn't know was why his aunt had left; what he did know was that she hadn't been spirited away by ghosts. There were no ghosts at Neddingfield Hall.

He didn't have time to ponder on who had left the horses; he was fully occupied keeping himself in the saddle and hanging on to the three he was leading. He became aware, as they approached the Hall, there was no longer any need to drag the Neddingfield mounts, they recognized they were approaching home and began to increase their pace, knowing a warm stall and good food awaited them.

This presented a problem of its own. The fourth time the horses surged forward, trying to rush past, causing a blockage in the narrow lane, Ralph decided to take action before one of them was hurt.

'All of you, release the leads; let them find their own way. It will be safer for all of us.'

The three men responded to his suggestion with alacrity. Ralph knew that their sleeves must be as full of snow as his, their boot tops also. In spite of his gloves his fingers were numb to the bone and hanging on to the lead rein had become increasingly difficult. His left arm felt as if it had been wrenched from its socket several times in the past hour. It was impossible to release the horses whilst still mounted. He remained where he was, leaving Robin to organize matters for him.

Grinning at his man's antics he took the opportunity to shake as much of the snow from his person as he could. 'I'll leave you in charge, Robin. I shall head back and let them know what to expect.' He looked round, whistling loudly. Jet loped into sight and together they set off towards the Hall.

Ralph considered what he had discovered. He knew he could have gone in and shaken a little more information out of the old man, but not enough to make to make such brutal treatment acceptable. He would never willingly harm those weaker than himself. He let Thunder have his head; the horse was as sure-footed and as eager to return as he was.

He had been through the study examining every piece of paper, but there was nothing there to give him a clue as to her whereabouts. He knew his cousin was right; they had been taken to the coast and embarked on a ship.

Like an icy chill, one piece of the puzzle unexpectedly fell into place. Was it possible the letters they had received summoning them to Neddingfield had not been written by his aunt? This was the one thing he hadn't checked. As soon as he got back he would find Aunt Agatha's diary and compare it with the letter he had in his room. Someone had wished to lure them both here. He glanced over his shoulder as if expecting to be ambushed at any moment.

Chapter Eight

HESTER WAS IN the study reading her aunt's diary when her cousin burst in.

'Good heavens, you're dripping wet! Aren't you going to change your clothes before joining me?'

He stopped and looked down at his mud-spattered britches then shook his head, grinning. 'If you've no objection, my dear, I shall remain as I am. I did take time to remove my greatcoat and gloves, which will have to suffice.'

Intrigued, she laid the book down, waiting to be enlightened.

'Is that Aunt Agatha's diary you have in front of you? It's what I came in to see.'

Hester noticed he had a square of folded paper in his hand and understood his mission. 'The letters, of course! They must be forgeries; nothing else makes sense. I'm afraid I don't have mine to compare, it's back at Draycot.'

He came across to join her by the desk, smoothing out the letter as he did so. She opened the book and waited expectantly for him to place it down. When he did so she felt a wave of disappointment.

'Oh dear, we're wrong. This is by the same hand. Look – the ink's identical, and I believe the same quill was used, I can see the blobs and splatters on the last page of the diary are the same as those in your letter.'

Ralph grabbed another straight-backed chair and brought it over so that he could sit next to her. 'I'm not so sure. There *are* differences. See, the S in the letter is quite different.' His finger stabbed at the letters and she felt a thrill of excitement.

'Yes, you're right and the signature is not quite the same either. If I recall correctly, Aunt Agatha always added a swirl underneath her name. There's none here.'

He slapped his hand on the desk making her jump. 'My God, you're right. This letter wasn't sent by Aunt Agatha, but by whoever spirited her away. At least one part of the puzzle is solved.'

His arm was pressing close to hers and she could feel his heat through her sleeve. She felt him still, and glanced upwards, seeing a strange expression on his face; then he was on his feet and striding up and down the carpet.

'Tell me, did you find the horses hidden somewhere near the coast?'

'I apologize, I should have said when I came in. It was exactly as you predicted. I came on ahead, but no doubt the animals are back in their stables now. Someone will have to ride in to town later, we're going to need more outside staff.'

'Please, won't you sit down and explain exactly what happened? I've been beside myself with curiosity these past two hours.'

When Ralph had finished his story she realized he had missed what could be a vital clue. 'The old man at the farm, he didn't seem surprised to see you?'

'No, that's true, he didn't. He was expecting someone to come back and reclaim the horses.'

She nodded encouragingly, waiting for him to reach the same conclusion. For a moment he looked blank then his mouth curled in a heart-stopping smile. 'You're there before me, once again. The man was expecting someone like me to arrive, so was not surprised when I hammered on his door. This tells us that whoever's behind this, is a member of the gentry.'

'That indeed narrows the list of suspects down. There can only be several thousand people to deal with, not several million.'

'I can think of no reason why anyone should wish to lure me here under false pretences.'

'However, you were. But we have not proved that my letter was false. In fact, I'm almost certain that it had the correct signature and the wording was quite different. Exactly when did you receive yours?'

'The day before I arrived, Aunt Agatha said the matter was of extreme urgency.'

'My invitation was of long standing; it was arranged weeks ago. Is it possible that whoever sent for you didn't know I was expected too?'

'This gets more complicated by the minute.'

She had been thinking about this and had come to the same conclusion from whichever direction she approached the problem. 'I think I might have an explanation. It's a trifle far-fetched, but then this whole scenario is bordering on the ridiculous. Do you wish to hear it?'

He was all attention, leaning forward, his expression expectant.

'It has to do with money, it always does,' she paused, 'or love, of course; sometimes it's to do with love.' She glanced up, eyes twinkling. 'I rather think an elopement can be ruled out in this case. I think it must be to do with your recent inheritance. Could there be someone else who had expectations? A man who wants the title and your fortune enough to kill you for it?'

As soon as she said the words out loud she felt as if a stone lodged in her stomach. Her eyes widened and the colour drained from her face. 'I'm right, aren't I? Someone has brought you here to kill you?' She looked fearfully around the room, as if expecting the murderer to appear from behind the curtain hangings. 'And as I'm here, they will have to kill me too, as I shall be a witness.'

Her startling announcement hung in the air between them, then Ralph was on his feet and at her side and she felt his arms around her, warm and comforting, and her fear began to subside.

'Kill us? What a nonsensical idea. You've been reading far too many Gothic novels, sweetheart, and they're making you fanciful. There'll be a far simpler explanation. It has nothing to do with murder or money.'

As Ralph gathered the shaking girl in his arms and spoke his words of comfort he was lying to her. She *was* correct. It had to be his inheritance. Both of them stood to gain on Aunt Agatha's demise, and now he also held a title and a massive fortune of his own.

He'd come to her side with the intention of offering reassurance; she was ten years his junior and, to him, seemed not much more than a green girl. But somehow, his body was telling him different. He felt her warmth, the softness of her breasts pressing against his shirt front and inhaling the sweet scent of her hair caused his body to respond accordingly.

This wouldn't do. He was her guardian, and he would not take advantage; it would be unpardonable. Releasing her he stepped away, turning his back to hide his embarrassment. He wandered across to gaze morosely out of the window, waiting for his arousal to subside.

There were enough complications at the moment without adding a growing attraction to his beautiful cousin. He straightened, his eyes narrowed and his face relaxed. Was it such an outlandish idea? Why not her? He was turned thirty, held an ancient title, what would make more sense than to marry his second cousin and keep the money in one place? This was the ideal opportunity to stake his claim. They were virtually unchaperoned, and he would have every opportunity to seduce her and make it impossible for her to say no to matrimony.

Hester watched him, puzzled by his sudden departure from her side. Had she done something to offend him? One moment she had been warm and safe, next rudely put aside and he had stalked off to stand on the far side of the room and stare out across the snow. She didn't know a great deal about men, didn't go often to public events, mostly to parties held by her intimates, but she knew enough to be aware of a slight, and didn't enjoy the experience at all. A growing anger at her shabby treatment replaced her fear and she stood up. Should she berate him for his rudeness?

She was standing, indecisively, when he swung back to face her, looking at her in a most disconcerting way. It was as if he was seeing her for the first time. She felt his glance linger on her face then travel swiftly down, across her heaving bosom to her toes. She responded by flushing pink all over. Why was he staring at her in this way and making her feel uncomfortable? She nodded regally, and turning her back on him departed in dignified silence. The last thing she wanted was for him to take an *interest* in her.

She shivered in the icy corridor, pulling her wrap close, and decided to go in search of Birdie. She remembered that the housekeeper had a small room of her own adjacent to the butler's pantry. The woman had used both rooms as her domain as there was no butler at Neddingfield.

The large house was divided into sections. The main part was used by Aunt Agatha, but the smaller wing, which made it into an L-shape, housed the various domestic offices, as well as the servants' hall; on the first floor were the butler and house-keeper's rooms. These could be accessed only by taking the back stairs.

It was even colder here, the walls were not lit by sconces, and you had to hold your own candlestick in order to see your way. Thankfully emerging in the correct place, Hester was pleased to see that there was a coal fire burning in the grate and the area was a lot warmer than the main part of the house. The door to the housekeeper's parlour was standing open and her friend was seated at a table writing meticulously in a large ledger. She hesitated at the door; might it be polite to knock? Birdie looked up, her plain face softened by a smile of welcome.

'My dear, whatever are you doing up here? You had only to ring, and someone would have fetched me down to see you.'

'I've no intention of allowing you to run after me. I told you, apart from a slight headache, I'm fully recovered and the exercise has done me good. I'm sure if I remained sedentary for long, with my prodigious appetite, I would get too fat to move, even if I wanted to.'

Birdie laughed, as she was meant to. 'Come in, you're very welcome. Actually, it's far warmer on our side of the house than it is on yours. I've had a tray of tea brought, and Cook included some fruit buns. I've finished here; I was just entering what we've used from the pantry today – it's the way things are done. I'm now free to join you by the fire.'

'Do you know, I've never been up here before. I had no idea it was so comfortable and well appointed. I doubt that many houses have such rooms for their staff. I can see now why you are so eager to become housekeeper; here you're warm and don't have to negotiate the icy corridors every time you want to move from room to room.'

'Very true, my dear. Now tell me what you've been doing this morning. One of the girls, Mary, told me the horses have been found and are now safe in the stables. That's good news, but confirms your theory that Miss Culley and her staff have taken a sea voyage. Was she in the habit of taking all her staff with her when she travelled?'

Hester held her tea, served in dainty porcelain, decorated in pink and edged in gilt. She was sure this was not the tea service normally used up here, whatever Birdie thought, the rest of the staff knew she wasn't really one of them.

'It's something I never asked. Why should I? Perhaps Polly might know, she was walking out with a young man who worked here. He could have mentioned he was going to travel with my aunt.'

They sipped their tea companionably. Hester devoured two of the freshly cooked buns liberally spread with butter. 'The more I think about it, the more odd it seems. They left the chickens, and the two house cows, but no one to feed or milk them. Surely if they'd planned to go away they would have made arrangements for the livestock? It's all very odd. I must discuss it with Colebrook.'

'Are you now assisting Lord Colebrook?'

Hester detected a smug satisfaction in her friend's voice and knew her suspicions that she was determined to make a match between them were correct. 'On the matter of Colebrook, I do not appreciate being thrown at his head. We're both quite capable of finding a partner, if that's what we desire. Are you hoping that our proximity will cause us to become compromised?'

The usual snort accompanied this comment. 'You could do far worse, my dear. You must own he's not an antidote. A trifle tall, I admit, but apart from that he's everything he should be. He would have no need of buckram wadding to improve the width of his shoulders or the shape of his calves. He's been a professional soldier all his life, I believe. I can't think of anyone better to take care of you.'

It was Hester's turn to snort. 'Birdie, he's definitely a man used to giving commands, that I will agree. *I* should not like to be tied to such a one; imagine being ordered, barked and shouted at all day. It wouldn't suit me. Admittedly having a professional soldier around at the moment is more than fortunate, but when this mystery is satisfactorily solved, I shall be quite happy to say farewell and send him on his way.'

She stood up, shaking the crumbs from her lap. 'I shan't require any luncheon after eating two buns, but if it's soup again I shall not be able to resist; yesterday it was delicious.'

She paused as an unpleasant thought occurred to her. 'Birdie, *this* cook is still preparing food for all the staff, is she not? The outside men as well? I couldn't bear to think of them going without in weather like this.'

Birdie nodded. 'But of course she is, my dear. Lord Colebrook insists on it. He has also given permission to light fires in their rooms above the stables, and to take any extra furniture and bedding that they might require to make their quarters snug and warm. He's a good man, my dear, and looks after his own. He's not like other aristocrats; he wasn't born into wealth, and has only inherited recently.'

Hester was finding this constant praise of her cousin tiresome. 'I must see how Polly's progressing with the alterations. What time is luncheon, at midday as usual?'

'Yes, my dear, but his lordship has asked that dinner be served at six, instead of five; it seems he prefers not to keep country hours.'

Ralph waited until he was alone before pacing the study, cursing his clumsiness. He mustn't rush matters, Hester, although turned twenty one, had not gone about in society. His aunt had told him she lived quietly with her companion, Miss Bird, at

Draycot Manor, managing her own estate and finances admirably. For all that, even to his untutored eye he could see she dressed to advantage. The gold velvet gown she had been wearing, in spite of its long sleeves and high neck, emphasized her delectable breasts, and added dignity to her slender frame. He couldn't wait to remove the pins and watch her hair tumble over her shoulders, the way it had when they first met.

He could see the sky was clear, no sign of heavy snow clouds, though the temperature was well below freezing and the snow showed no sign of thawing. Robin had told him there was enough fodder and bedding stored to last the winter, the barns full of sweet-smelling hay, barley straw, and sacks of oats. The cellars beneath the kitchen were crammed full of carrots, potatoes, onions, preserves and jars of fruit. There were sides of ham, bacon, salt beef, and other delicacies. With the chickens, the house cows, and what could be shot in the woods, no one would go hungry however long they were obliged to stay here. Even the coal cellar was full. The house was stocked for winter: his aunt had not intended to go away. What could have persuaded her to leave as she did? Hester could be correct, perhaps her arrival was an unfortunate coincidence.

His mouth curved involuntarily as he pictured her bristling with indignation before stalking out. Whatever the reason, he was glad she was here. They might not have met otherwise, but having to keep both her and her companion safe was an added complication.

He frowned. Too much time was being spent thinking about his cousin. It had to stop: there were more pressing things for him to do.

What they required were more servants; the dozen women already employed formed no more than a skeleton staff in a house this size. Another dozen would not go amiss and there was ample room in the attics, and sufficient food to feed any extra.

Outside they needed at least two more grooms, two more gardeners and a couple of handymen. He would feel more sanguine if he had half-a-dozen men able to handle firearms as well. Although he had dismissed his cousin's worries, he believed things could get decidedly unpleasant before this matter ended.

He walked to the wall and yanked the bell. Eventually there was a knock on the door and James appeared, looking a little shamefaced.

'Forgive me, my lord, when the bell rang I took this opportunity of coming myself. I would like to speak to you.'

'Excellent, it was you I wished to see. I want you to try and ride to town; the snow's deep, but there's a route through the wood which is more sheltered. You can cut through and approach Little Neddingfield from the rear. It's the way those intruders must have entered and left the park. Go to the inn and recruit more staff. I have my requirements written.' He handed over the note. 'With the price of corn so high even basic foodstuffs must be out of reach of the unemployed farm labourers of the neighbourhood, so I hope they will be happy to come. Do you think you can you make the journey safely?'

'I do, my lord. My horse is well rested, and if I toss a blanket over its rump, I'm sure we can get there and back. However, I'm not sure that many folk, however needy, will want to trudge four miles through the snow in order to get here. It's a pity it's so thick or I could take a wagon with me and bring them back on that.'

Ralph frowned, this was one aspect of the situation that bothered him. It was likely many of the people who volunteered to work would be poorly clad and not have weatherproof footwear. He couldn't expect them to walk in the snow, however eager he was to employ them.

'Well, I suggest you go anyway. Book yourself a room at the inn; it will probably take you a day or two to round up the number of people I want, and by then, the weather might have improved, and they can walk ... No, on second thoughts, hire a diligence, and bring them out on that. I don't want anything unpleasant to happen on *this* journey; I don't know what we're dealing with here.'

James nodded. 'I'll pack my saddle-bags, and set off right away, my lord. With luck, if I don't fall into any drifts, I'll be there before dark. I won't be able to send word to you, but expect me back, snow or no snow, with the required staff within two days.'

The young man departed and Ralph realized they had not discussed the reason that had brought James to him in the first place. He shrugged. Pulling out a chair at the desk, he rubbed his eyes, trying to clear his head, there were things that needed to be thought about and here was as good a place as any.

There were far too many unexplained events and if he was of a fanciful turn of mind he would begin to think supernatural forces *were* involved. There was only one way to sift the facts from fantasy: he would write it down. He selected a quill, uncorked the ink and began.

Questions to be answered:
1. *The gates were closed and no one to have done it*
2. *Occupants of Neddingfield Hall vanish without trace*
3. *Mysterious camp with no footprints visible*
4. *Man vanishes without trace in the wood.*

Answers to questions:
1. *They could have been closed by whoever took the Neddingfield occupants away. Not ghosts.*
2. *Horses found, evidence of ex-soldiers. Not ghosts.*
3. *Camp, the footprints could have been removed, but not clear how. Ghosts?*
4. *Vanished man, no explanation. Ghosts?*

He perused his paper carefully, writing it down hadn't helped him at all. There must be a rational explanation so why hadn't he found it? There were no ghosts at Neddingfield Hall; whatever was happening here was almost certainly orchestrated by a human hand. He was damned if he was going to start believing in the supernatural.

Chapter Nine

Until the snow melted Ralph couldn't post the letter to his lawyers in London asking them if they knew who his heir was, and the militia would not get through. Nothing more could be done to further his investigations. He felt frustrated; he was a man of action and wanted to get on with things, not sit around waiting for the weather to improve.

The sound of shouts and laughing outside attracted his attention. His cousin was up to her knees in snow, so muffled by garments he scarcely recognized her. She was accompanied by two gardeners holding shovels and was obviously intending to build a snowman. Good grief! The girl had taken leave of her senses. He watched, smiling at her inadequate attempts to construct the torso. She needed an expert to help her.

He ran up to his chambers, found his heavy riding coat and gloves, then, tying a scarf around his neck, he bounded downstairs and went to join the fun. It was years since he had thought of the snow as anything but an inconvenience. By the time four figures were completed he believed his relationship with his cousin had improved somewhat and that she no longer considered him an irascible ogre.

The physical activity had allowed him to expend his pent-up energy, and he returned to the study in a better frame of mind. This evening they were to dine together for the first time and

Hester had told him she was going to dress for dinner. He smiled, he hadn't worn the evening rig hanging in his closet and it would make a refreshing change not to appear in his scarlet regimentals.

Hester examined her new gown from all angles, craning her neck to see how it fell without its train.

'I can't believe it's the same garment, Polly. You've worked wonders. The ruffles added around the hem make it the first stare of fashion. I wish I had thought to bring my jewellery with me, as the *décolletage* is too revealing.' She glanced down nervously at the expanse of creamy bosom exposed above the neckline.

'No, Miss Frobisher, it looks lovely. With your hair dressed, and ringlets on either side of your face, you look just like the picture in the book. I'm sure Lord Colebrook will appreciate the effort you've taken.'

Hester's mouth pursed. 'I dress to please myself, Polly, not anyone else.' The reprimand was unfair and she tried to make amends. 'I do thank you. But it's one thing to look like a sophisticate, and quite another to maintain the pretence all evening.' She nodded to her young abigail. 'I shall leave the rest of my wardrobe in your capable hands. If Meg helps I believe the contents of my closet can be made over. It might be more difficult with the gowns that don't have a high waistline, but the skirts of those are so full there should be enough to make a fresh gown. Do you have enough thread and trimmings?'

The girl nodded. 'Yes, thank you, miss. The box you found for me has everything I want. I could sew you a complete wardrobe without needing more.'

After a final check, Hester enveloped herself in a warm cashmere shawl knowing she would need it to negotiate the icy passageways. The tall clock that stood in pride of place in the grand hall, struck six as she reached the top of the staircase. Carefully lifting the hem of her silk gown she ran down lightly, not wishing to be tardy tonight.

The drawing-room door was open, the room ablaze with candlelight; the chandelier in the centre sparkled like the snow outside. She paused, unconsciously framing herself in the doorway, unaware of the impact she was making. Colebrook was waiting, his back to the fire, for her arrival.

She gazed down the length of the room. Her throat closed. In black, apart from his shirt front, the silver of his waistcoat and the frothy whiteness of his intricately tied cravat, which was held in place by a single diamond pin, he looked magnificent. He looked every inch an aristocrat. Whatever his words to the contrary, he was born to rule.

She took a few hesitant steps, then dropped in a low curtsy. Gracefully she straightened and watched him bow deeply in return. No words were spoken, but the silence said more than banalities could ever do.

Ralph found his voice first and moved smoothly towards her, his hand extended. 'Good evening, Cousin Hester. Permit me to say that you look enchanting tonight, my dear.'

'And you look ... you look overwhelming. Evening dress suits you, but it does emphasize your height in an alarming way.' She felt a strange tingle travel up her fingers as he took her hand and threaded it through his arm.

'I believe dinner is served. Shall we go through?'

He led her with as much formality as if progressing at the grandest state occasion, halfway down the length of the drawing-room, through the double doors that led to the dining-room, and across to the huge table that dominated the centre of the room.

Hester was relieved to see that Birdie had not placed them at either end of the table so that they would have been obliged to shout to each other in order to converse. The two places were side by side, near the sideboard upon which the various courses were waiting. A trio of nervous parlour-maids were ready to serve.

'Allow me, my dear.' He pulled out a chair and waited while she stepped round, then pushed it in as if he'd been acting as a footman all his life. With a flourish he removed her intricately folded napkin and shook it out, placing it across her lap. She smiled, enjoying his performance.

He seated himself with less fuss and indicated they were ready to be served. He poured her a glass of claret. Hester was not used to drinking alcohol; in fact, apart from the occasional glass of champagne at weddings and at Christmas, she avoided it. She disliked the way it made her head spin and her senses became confused. She also disliked the way it changed people, making them loud, red-faced and embarrassingly uninhibited.

Ralph watched her sip her drink with distaste and snapped his fingers to have her glass removed and replaced by lemonade. He made sure to be at his most charming, telling her amusing anec-dotes about his time on the Peninsula and the frolics of his fellow officers. As the meal progressed it became more obvious that all animosity between them was gone.

'My dear, I have been doing all the talking. It is your turn to tell me about yourself, how you come to be of age but still unmarried.' He saw her smile slip and realized this was not a subject she wished to discuss with him.

'I am happy to regale you with stories of my youth, but that is all. You have no right to question me on such a personal matter.'

Dammit! He'd made a mull of it. It was too long since he'd been obliged to do the pretty with an innocent. How could he restore himself in her eyes without looking like a nincompoop?

'I beg your pardon, Hester, you're quite right to castigate me. The subject is closed. Now, I am all agog to hear what you got up to at Draycot Manor.'

When the final remove was taken from the table he was ready, rising smoothly to be at her side to assist her from her chair. As he stood behind her, looking over her shoulder, he felt the all-too-familiar tightness. She was so beautiful and dressed as she was in this gold silk evening gown she was damn near irresistible.

He knew if he made his advance too soon, he would scare her, but it was becoming almost impossible to behave as a gentleman with so much temptation at his fingertips. Carefully avoiding any contact with her bare shoulders he pulled her chair back, allowing her to slip sideways, away from his grasp. She moved to the far end of the room, looking at him warily. Did she suspect what he had in mind? He banked down the fire in his eyes before speaking.

'Shall we go through into the drawing-room, my dear? I have no wish to sit on my own imbibing port when I can be talking to the most beautiful woman in England.'

He saw a faint pink colour her cheeks at his fulsome compliment and for a moment felt ashamed. She was no match for him; he was experienced in the ways of the world and knew exactly how to further his suit.

Why was he looking at her as though he wished to devour her? She'd enjoyed sharing dinner with him, listening to his stories and, apart from his intrusive questions about her single state, the evening had gone splendidly. Having spent all morning building snowmen with him she had revised her opinion, and was coming to almost like him.

Would it be wise to spend any further time in his company? She had observed him refill his glass, and knew from watching the brothers and husbands of her friends, that men did things they might later regret, when in their cups.

She nodded coolly; she didn't want to give him any encouragement. 'My lord, I have enjoyed this evening, but you will forgive me, I'm sure, if I retire to my chambers. It's been a long day, and, as you know, I spent the greater part of the morning in physical activity outside, and I'm feeling decidedly fatigued.'

She saw his mouth tighten so played her trump card. 'I believe I'm not quite as well as I thought. After all, Dr Ratcliff did say I should remain in my room for another day after the …' She paused to give her next remark more impact. 'After my unfortunate accident a few days ago.'

He frowned. 'Of course. Shall I ring for someone to escort you to your chambers?'

Before he could reach the bell she raised her hand to halt him. 'There's no need. I feel tired and my head aches a little, but I'm quite capable of seeing myself upstairs.'

Believing she was safe, at least for tonight, she gathered her skirts and prepared to leave. Then somehow he was close behind her, his hot breath brushing the top of her head.

'I believe you will need your wrap to negotiate the corridors. Allow me to place it on your shoulders.'

She felt the whisper of the fine material as it dropped across her neck and then his hands brushed her cheeks as he delicately folded it around her. She couldn't move. His proximity was making her head spin. He was so overwhelmingly masculine.

Eventually she found her voice, and even to her it sounded shaky and unnatural. 'Thank you, sir, that's most kind.' She attempted to step forward but for some reason her feet wouldn't move, she was rooted, trapped by something she didn't understand.

Strong fingers closed on her shoulders and slowly she was turned to face him. She stood trembling within the circle of his arms, no more than a hand span between them, and she wasn't sure if she shook with fear or something else entirely.

'Look at me, Hester, sweetheart, please.'

His voice was hypnotic, and she couldn't prevent herself. She tilted her head and her lips parted in invitation. She took an involuntary step backwards only to find her retreat prevented by his arms. She knew what he intended, knew that half of her longed to feel his mouth on hers, experience her first kiss, but the other half screamed a warning.

Once she had tasted his lips, she would be lost, her freedom compromised, and before she knew what was happening he would be on one knee making an offer that she would be in no position to refuse. She had no option; there was only one way out of this impasse: she closed her eyes and allowed herself to collapse in a silken heap at his feet.

Ralph could feel his heart thundering, knew her capitulation was imminent. He had to kiss her, to place his mouth over hers, taste its sweetness, crush her to him. He'd never felt this way, so out of control, like a lovesick boy not a man of two and thirty. He watched her eyes widen – saw the invitation – knew this was the moment.

He relaxed his hold, preparing to pull her closer but she slipped through his fingers. Too late. His reactions were slow, far too slow, and to his horror she lay in a puddle of gold, unconscious on the floor.

Swearing under his breath, disgusted that his behaviour had caused her to swoon, he scooped her up and, cradling her next to his heart, carried her upstairs to her rooms. The two maidservants greeted him with barely concealed opprobrium and reluctantly he left his love in their capable hands. He stomped back to the study with the intention of drinking himself into oblivion, ashamed that he had allowed his base nature to overcome his better judgment.

What the hell was the matter with him? Why did the proximity of his cousin make him behave like a coxcomb?

*

Hester remained still, stretched out on the day-bed, until she heard the distinctive click of the door closing. Immediately she raised her head. 'Has he gone? Is it safe for me to recover?' She sat up, laughing at the shocked expressions on their faces. 'It was a sham, I could think of nothing else to avoid ... well it seemed the best way in the circumstances.'

She saw the two girls exchange glances and understood that they were better versed in the wicked ways of gentlemen than she was. Polly leant down and offered her hand.

'Please, Miss Frobisher, let me help you to your feet. You'll spoil your gown if you lie down in it for much longer.'

The lovely garment was hung in the closet where she thought it might be better if it remained. She had escaped unscathed this time, but she didn't think she would be so lucky if she was fool-hardy enough to appear dressed in a gown that was obviously such an invitation to a man like him.

Before she got into bed she decided to look at the snowmen they'd built outside on the lawn. Taking the candlestick, she pulled aside the curtain, opening the shutter a little to look out. The hair on her forearms stood up and her mouth went dry. Across the park in the woods lights were floating, some high some low; they appeared one moment and the next they'd gone. She slammed the shutter, dropped the curtain and sped back across the carpet to scramble into bed.

Shaking from cold and fear, the candle snuffed and the room was dark. The fire banked up for the night threw little light into the room and she was too scared to climb out and rekindle her candle. She wriggled down, pulling the comforter over her head in an effort to block out the memory of the ghostly lights.

Gradually her pulse returned to normal and, as her terror abated, common sense returned. Hadn't her cousin told her the area was used by free-traders? Yes. That was what she'd witnessed, nothing demonic about it, merely smugglers returning from the coast with illegal goods.

Deliberately relaxing, her thoughts turned to pleasanter things. She wasn't sure how she felt about her first experience of intimacy, but knew Ralph had intended to kiss her and certain his actions were wrong, that he was treating her with disrespect. The fact that she had wanted him to was neither here nor there – he was a gentleman; it was up to him to restrain himself.

Just because they were being thrown into each other's company didn't mean he could take liberties with her person. She might be an innocent, but even she knew that only couples who were betrothed were allowed to indulge in such intimacies. She shuddered. He might be ready to give up his freedom, but she was certain she was not. She smiled drowsily. If she was thinking of matrimony the last person she would choose would be Lord Colebrook. He was far too controlling.

Halfway down his second decanter of cognac Ralph felt he was ready to sleep. Not bothering to stagger upstairs, as Robin would have taken to his bed long ago and not be there to assist him, he removed his evening jacket and tossed it carelessly on the desk. Stretching out on the mat in front of the fire, he yawned, his only concession to comfort a cushion he'd snatched from one of the leather armchairs.

The fire was high, the carpet far more comfortable than many places he'd rested his head over the years. He slept soundly for the first time since he'd arrived at Neddingfield; the alcohol he'd consumed helping with his slumbers. His dreams were disturbed by a furious banging, but he ignored it. Then someone was shaking his shoulder and he was rudely jerked awake.

'My lord, dreadful news, please, you must come at once.'

Instantly alert, in spite of the quantities of claret and cognac he'd drunk the night before, he sprung to his feet, shocked by the expression on Robin's face.

'What is it, man? Tell me.'

'It's James, my lord. He never reached town, at least we don't think he did, his horse staggered into the yard just now, half dead with cold.'

'Oh hell! Let's assume he's had a fall, not imagine the worst. Give me five minutes; I can hardly come out dressed as I am.' He heard Robin thundering up the stairs behind him and was glad his man had thought to follow. It would be far quicker to disrobe and put on his britches and boots if he had assistance. Ten minutes later he was in the kitchen, draining a cup of coffee. Snatching a chunk of newly baked bread, he pulled on his heavy riding coat, jammed his beaver on his head, and ran outside.

In the stable, Tom, and one of the local men, were doing their best for the horse, but after a cursory glance, he thought the animal was unlikely to survive. Thoroughbreds could not withstand the cold and this poor beast had obviously been up to his belly in snow most of the night. It would be kinder to shoot it now, but he didn't have time for it.

'Where's the tack? I want to see the saddle and bridle; it's possible I can discover something you missed.'

These were fetched and he took them outside into the early morning light to get a closer look. His jaw clenched in anger. The grooms had missed a vital clue in their desperation to get the horse warm; there was a smear of blood across the pommel. As the horse had not been injured, it could only mean one thing.

'This is not good, Robin, in fact it's bloody bad. The boy must have met with an accident. Pray he hasn't frozen to death overnight.'

Chapter Ten

'IT SHOULD BE easy enough to follow the tracks of the horse back into the wood, my lord. Shall I arm the men and saddle the horses?'

'Not yet, Robin. Five more minutes isn't going to make much difference either way.' James was one of Hester's men, had been with her for several years; she would be devastated if anything untoward had happened. He was tempted to go inside and explain, but decided against it. Knowing her, she would insist on coming with them, and her health was not robust enough to be outside on horseback.

He was reduced to two armed men, plus four outdoor servants, who could, at a push, wield a cudgel. He had a horrible suspicion his men were being removed one by one; if he wasn't careful he would be isolated. He stared up at the grey clouds rapidly approaching from the coast. Within an hour or two it would be snowing; if he was going to look for the boy, he had to do it now, not stand around procrastinating.

Decision made, he strode back into the stable to find Robin waiting at the heads of the two horses he'd chosen. If the situation hadn't been so dire he would have smiled. These were not thoroughbreds, but workhorses, ones that pulled a farm wagon.

'I thought these would do better in the snow, my lord. We've probably lost one, I don't want to lose any more.'

Ralph turned to the four men, sacks tied round their legs with string, inadequate coats buttoned across their chests and stringy mufflers around their necks. All wore caps dragged down to cover their ears. He couldn't, in all conscience, allow them to come out in a possible blizzard. 'You four, I no longer wish you to accompany me. Get shovels and clear the walkways, if further snow falls this area will be dangerous in the extreme.'

The largest touched his forelock and grinned. 'A bit of snow won't 'urt us, me lord. We're 'appy enough to follow you, if you think it'd 'elp.'

'No, I thank you, I shall go with my man. We're both armed, and better dressed to brave the elements.'

One of the four jumped forward, pushing open the arched doors, and Ralph trotted out. The wind was not as icy as before, but he knew it didn't herald a change in the weather, unfortunately.

He directed his sturdy mount to the trail the returning horse had left. At times the snow was up to its chest, but it didn't seem to bother the beast, it just poked its nose forward and ploughed on. Ralph patted the animal's neck.

The trail led them into a clearing just in front of the five-barred gate that marked the end of the wood and then stopped abruptly. No hoofprints the other side of the gate, nothing to show that anyone apart from James and his mount had been there. The young man would have had to jump the gate, or dismount to open it. It was here that he would have had his mind on other things.

'This could be where he was taken.' Ralph looked over his shoulder, searching the undergrowth, and surroundings, for signs of an ambush. There was none and his instincts told him they were quite alone in this desolate place. If someone had been here they were long gone. He looked around for evidence but saw nothing.

'Dismount, Robin, and search properly. I'm certain we're at the spot he was taken, but from up here I can see nothing suspicious. If I was inclined to be superstitious I'd say something unnatural has occurred here. This is the second man who has vanished without trace with no evidence of human intervention.'

He waited for Robin to laugh, but the man turned away unsmiling. Ralph knew he had not mistaken the look of fear on his companion's face. They had fought side by side throughout many bloody campaigns and this was the first time he'd seen him unsettled.

He lowered himself to the ground, not wishing to fill his boots with snow. There was no necessity to tether his mount, as it seemed content to stand. The animal, a nondescript brown, lowered its massive head and blew clouds of warmth down the back of his neck. He reached up and rubbed the hairy muzzle.

'Good fellow, you stand here. I promise we'll not keep you waiting long and then you shall return and have a large bucket of oats for your trouble.'

They quartered the area, the way they did as serving soldiers, but found nothing: no blood, no helpful threads of red coat, nothing to say that James had been there at all. He straightened, shaking his head in disappointment.

'We're going to find nothing here, Robin. At least I can tell Miss Frobisher he appears to have been taken, not killed. That will be some consolation.' But by whom or what he wasn't sure. He saw Robin's apprehension and realized his choice of words had been inopportune, merely reinforcing his suspicion that unworldly forces were at work.

A flurry of white brushed across his cheek and he looked up dismayed to see the clouds had arrived quicker than he'd antici-pated. 'We'd better hurry, or we'll be stuck out here in a blizzard.'

He vaulted into the saddle, digging his heels into the horse's hairy flanks, then rammed his feet into the irons. Neither animal needed encouragement to return and they clattered back into the cobbled yard in good time. They had been riding blind for the last mile. Their arrival was heard and the doors swung open and he walked straight in.

'Thank God, I thought you'd left it too late, my lord. The weather's turned right nasty out there.' Tom's tone reflected his concern.

'We'd not be back at all if it hadn't been for these two nags. They knew their way home and all we had to do was keep our heads down and hang on.'

Ralph dropped to the floor sending a cloud of snow over the men standing closest. He looked round at their expectant faces. 'We found nothing, and in some ways that's good news. James has been abducted, taken somewhere else, but at least he's not dead.' One man stepped forward and led away his horse. 'Give both horses a bucket of oats – they deserve it.'

Hester joined Birdie in her comfortable rooms above the kitchen, it being the warmest place in the house. She told her friend what had transpired the previous night and how she had managed to extricate herself from a potentially damaging situation. She wasn't sure if Birdie was impressed or scandalized.

'Look, it's snowing again. The girl who brought us the tray said that Colebrook and his man haven't returned. Whatever possessed him go out in this weather?'

'I've no idea, but no doubt he'll explain it all to you when he returns. Remember, my dear, he's a veteran and well used to dealing with weather far worse than this.'

Hester had to be satisfied with this answer, but she was restless all morning, unable to settle to anything. She had begun to feel uneasy at Neddingfield; for some strange reason she felt trapped within its walls. She returned to her seat beside the fire and munched quietly on the feather-light biscuits Cook had sent up to accompany their mid-morning refreshment. She could not sit up here doing nothing; she would go out to the stables and see what was going on.

'Thank you for the coffee and conversation, but I must return to my chambers to see how the alterations are progressing. It will be delightful to have another gown to wear during the day, for this is the third day I have been obliged to wear this one.'

'My dear, it's a good thing it suits you so well. Cook is coming up with today's menu in a moment, so I should have had to ask you to leave.'

Hester's eyebrows raised. Ask her to leave? Her companion was usually docility itself, and wouldn't dream of suggesting her employer leave, whatever the reason. Smiling to herself, she clattered back down the stairs and out into the corridor that led to the kitchen, aware that these unusual circumstances seemed to be making them all behave out of character.

She would need to return to her apartment to put on outdoor clothing before she could venture to the stables. She hesitated – there were cloaks and clogs hanging next to the boot room, should she borrow those? Deciding it would save valuable time if she used a servant's cloak, she pushed open the door. As she did so the back door opened and a blast of icy snow enveloped her and she found herself face-to-face with a giant snowman.

For second she was taken aback. 'Good heavens, I'm relieved to see you back. I was about to come out the stables to enquire after you.'

'Then I'm glad you didn't, it's abominable out there. Go back to the study. We have things to talk about and it's far too cold to stand around here, dressed as you are.'

Obediently she turned back. He was right; she was already starting to feel chilled. Her dress was of heavy stuff, but it was not suited to the extreme conditions they were experiencing.

In the warmth of the study she paced, wondering how long it

would take him to remove his outer garments, clean his boots and brush down his britches. After twenty minutes her curiosity was replaced by annoyance. She didn't like to be left standing, even by a lord! Whatever could be keeping him? If she could change her clothes in less than ten minutes, surely a man could do the same. It was typical of him to disregard her feelings in this way.

She heard footsteps approaching and sat, straight-backed, behind the desk. Placing the bulk of this between them made her feel less vulnerable. The door swung open and he marched in, no apology, his face grim. She feared what was coming would be bad news.

'Sit down. Take the chair closest to the fire. You must be frozen after venturing out this morning.' She was pleased her voice sounded even, glad he couldn't see her clenched hands.

He nodded and sat down, moving the chair sideways, away from the fire, so that he was facing her. 'I'm afraid I've bad news for you: James has been abducted.'

'James? What do you mean? Why should anyone wish to kidnap James? How do you know this?' Her voice was shrill. It was too much coming as it did after her scare last night.

'His horse returned this morning without him, half dead with cold. I went out to look but we found no sign. He's vanished. His tracks ended by the gate that leads into the lane and we didn't find evidence of other horses, but I'm still sure he was ambushed.'

Her eyes filled. First Aunt Agatha then James – what was happening? She felt as if she was being dragged into a nightmare. 'Do you think they took him to prevent him bringing extra staff here to help us?'

'I can think of no other explanation, but I'm almost sure he's still alive.'

Hester brushed her tears away. 'I should hope so, indeed. I'm uneasy about these strange disappearances. Don't you think it's odd?' She remembered what she'd seen the night before and felt nauseous. 'Last night I saw lights in the woods. I thought they were smugglers, but after what happened to James I'm beginning to have grave doubts.'

'Doubts? Surely *you're* not considering the supernatural? I thought you were made of sterner stuff.' He shrugged, smiling at her, stood and began to stroll across the room. She forgot her worries, forgot everything apart from the man who was moving in her direction. Even the desk did not seem big enough to protect her.

'Please, Cousin, sit down. You are overlarge to be looming over a person like this.' Her words halted him and the fierce gleam in his eyes vanished to be replaced by a bland smile.

'I apologize, my dear. Shall I sit here by the desk, or will you join me by the fire? I promise not to alarm you further by *looming*.'

'I'm quite content where I am. But you would do better by the fire.'

The humour left his face and she regretted her sharp tongue. Hastily she tried to deflect his ire. 'I have come to the conclusion that Polly might possibly hold the key to this. If we can fathom out why she was attacked when the others were left unmolested, then we might be closer to an answer.'

'Then fetch the girl and let me question her.'

He turned to stare into the fire, rudely turning his back. Hester remained where she was, determined not to be sent running on an errand like a child. For a few minutes the only sound was the fire and the wind rattling the window frames.

Without turning he spoke again. 'I believe that I asked you to fetch your maid. I do not wish to repeat my request.'

His threat was veiled, but it would be foolish to disobey. She slammed back her chair and without a word stalked across the study and out into the icy corridor. A gentleman would not have suggested she fetch Polly, but would have rung for a servant or even gone himself.

She scampered up the main stairs and ran pell-mell along the corridor bursting into her parlour. 'Polly, are you in there? Lord Colebrook and I would like you to come downstairs; we have some questions to ask you.'

The girl jumped up spilling her sewing on to the carpet. 'Miss Frobisher, I hope that I haven't offended in any way?'

'No, of course you haven't. I'm delighted with you; in fact, I'm not going to let you go. You do realize I'm going to insist that you accompany me back to Draycot Manor?'

Hester saw the delight on Polly's face then watched it fade to sadness.

'Thank you, miss, I should've loved to come. Having employment with someone like you is something I've dreamed of, but I can't leave without my Sam.'

'Then I shall employ him as well. Come along, Polly, his lordship is waiting.' She didn't add that in his tetchy mood it would do neither of them any good to dawdle upstairs. She was tempted to detour to the kitchen, make the objectionable man kick his heels for a while longer, then, remembering the steely tone in which he'd issued his second instructions, thought better of it.

'Here we are, my lord. I *do* hope we have not kept you waiting.' Hester's tone dripped insincerity. Her false smile slipped under his hard stare.

'Polly, come and sit down. Take the chair by the desk. Don't look so worried, I just want to talk to you about your connection with Neddingfield Hall.'

The girl dipped in a low curtsy, walked quickly to the designated place where she sat, hands neatly in her lap, her head bowed demurely. Hester resumed her seat behind the desk wishing she could hide under it instead. She decided she would remain mute and not give him the opportunity to snap at her.

'Polly, we know that you're betrothed to a groom here, Sam Foster, do we have that right?'

She nodded. 'Yes, my lord, but we're not exactly betrothed. We can't think about getting wed until he finds himself a job as head groom and gets married accommodation along with it.'

'We think that whoever caused Miss Culley to leave here last week believes you know something you could reveal to us and that's why they tried to abduct you. Can you think what that might be?'

The girl stared at Ralph in astonishment. 'No, my lord, I can't. I've never been here, not until I came the other day. Although my Sam talked about the place, told me everything that was going on, and we often laughed about—' She stopped and Hester saw her flush painfully and longed to reassure her.

'What sort of things did he tell you, Polly?' Hester forgot her determination not to interrupt. Ralph flicked her a glance and she closed her mouth hastily. She was surprised her maid had not picked up on the tension.

'He told me once that Miss Culley had friends in France, not aristocrats you understand, but more the revolutionaries. She certainly went abroad and had plenty of foreign visitors. She had a captain with a fine yacht who used to come and collect her when the tides were right. Do you think that's where she's gone now?'

'It seems the most likely explanation. Do you know if Miss Culley travelled with her staff when she went away?'

'I think so, my lord. Usually she liked to take her own people. But my Sam said that she always arranges for a tenant farmer to come in and take care of the horses and so on whilst they're away. When she went last time she didn't bar the gates. That's the talk of the town, I can tell you. Gates shut and no one there to have done it.' The girl shivered dramatically at the thought. 'Something's not right here. People think—'

'Thank you, Polly, you have been most helpful. You may go now. I'm sure you have duties to attend to upstairs.'

'Yes, my lord.' She jumped to her feet eager to escape from the room.

Hester called her back. 'Polly, could you go to the kitchen and take a tray up for Miss Bird's luncheon?'

'Yes, miss, it'd be a pleasure.'

The door closed behind the girl leaving Hester bracing herself for a severe set down. To her relief Ralph smiled.

'I think Aunt Agatha might have supported Bonaparte, and not the English during the war.'

'Are you suggesting that she's run away?'

'It's possible. If someone discovered her sympathies they could have used it to blackmail her into leaving.'

Hester jumped to her feet. 'It's too preposterous. Aunt is a well-known freethinker, a Liberal, but not a traitor. I won't believe it.'

Chapter Eleven

IT WAS AS cold inside as it was out and the only room that was bearable at Bracken Manor was the drawing-room in which Bertram Sinclair spent most of his time. The fire burnt day and night, but the rest of the house was left to freeze. He had had his bed set up at the far end of the room, with bamboo screens to give him privacy.

He hated Lord Colebrook with a virulence he could scarcely contain. It was eating him up inside, and until the man was dead and the money and title returned to their rightful owner, himself, he would get no peace.

A loud bang on the door interrupted his vengeful thoughts and he smoothed out his face and ordered whoever it was to come in. He was expecting a message to have come from the woods that morning.

'Beggin' your pardon, sir, I 'ave the message you bin awaitin'.'

'For God's sake don't stand with the door open, close it, it's cold enough in here already.'

The man shuffled forward, wearing sacks tied round his legs, two coats and a muffler about his head; it obviously wasn't any warmer in the kitchens.

'It's like this, sir, they sent someone from the 'all through the woods; 'e didn't know what 'it 'im. The boys as took 'im found these papers in 'is pocket.'

Bertram reached out his hand and took the papers by the edge not wishing to stand any closer to the vermin-infested creature who was addressing him so familiarly. He no longer recognized the three men who had accompanied him from the New World.

Quickly perusing the first sheet he glanced up at the wretched man who was edging closer which meant he had to back away to stand in the howling draught from the leaky windows. Neddingfield was sending for more staff and there was a letter addressed to the militia and one to a legal firm in London. Not bothering to open those, just tossing them into the fire to watch them shrivel up, he felt a rush of triumph. He was in charge; and he had thwarted his enemies' plans yet again.

'Is that all?' Why didn't this object remove himself? His malodorous body was tainting the atmosphere. The business of the captive had to be dealt with.

'Does the man still live?'

'Yes, sir, 'e does at the moment. They thought it 'ud be useful to let him go later, 'alf mad with fear, thinking 'e 'ad been 'eld by ghosts in 'ell itself. Or they can top 'im, no problem, if that's what you wants.'

Bertram considered the suggestion. 'It would do no harm to keep him alive for the present. You're sure he has no idea where he is, or how he got there?'

'Yes, sir, Jonesie said 'e wos still unconscious, and trussed up like a fowl. They've stowed 'im be'ind some barrels. The lads says they'll moan and groan like, and rattle the chains every now and again just to keep 'im scared witless. The prisoner'll survive down there a few days I reckon.'

'Very well, is there anything else?'

The man shifted uncomfortably from side to side and Bertram felt his rage return; he had bad news. He didn't like bad news.

'It's like this, your 'onour, the staff 'ave run away. All them lights and the bangin' and clankin' the lads bin making was too much for 'em and they're on their way back to town.'

Bertram scowled, this was good news surely? 'That's exactly what I wanted; word will spread like wildfire around the neighbourhood and no one will dare come near Neddingfield Hall. Even if they think Colebrook is in some sort of danger, they'll not come to investigate, not if they think it's ghosts involved.'

'One of our lads over'eard 'em talking; it seems there's two ladies living there as well, one of 'em is an heir to the old lady wot wos livin' there.'

Bertram turned and swept the tray of congealing food and the empty decanter from the table. Then he stamped on the remains, crushing the glass and crockery to small shards. He didn't hear the door close or notice the man who had once been the closest thing he'd had to a friend, vanish back to the kitchen.

Another visitor? He had been planning this for over a year; how could he not have discovered that there was a second heir to Neddingfield Hall? He didn't like killing women; he did it, of course, but it wasn't something he enjoyed. But there could be no witnesses to his perfidy, this mystery woman's days were numbered. His men had instructions to continue to reduce morale with more ghostly goings-on and then in a day or two he would strike.

Hester collapsed at the desk, dropping her face in her hands. She loved her aunt, admired her defiance of convention, but this? It was too much to take in. Surprised Ralph hadn't spoken, she sat up to find him watching her from across the wooden surface.

He looked so fatigued, his face grey, his eyes bloodshot, then she understood he was equally shocked. She rallied and forced her mouth into a semblance of a smile. 'It seems plausible, does it not, that our aunt sailed to France for *some* reason?'

'It does indeed.' He paused, rubbing his eyes as if they ached.

'I wonder, my dear, as we have been in each other's company so much over the past two days, do you think we might dispense with formality? Shall we call each other by our given names?'

Hester was about to refuse, but how could defying convention in this small way matter after the revelations about their aunt? That she was in all likelihood a traitor. 'Very well, it's a trifle cumbersome referring to you as *Cousin Ralph*. You do realize, that by being on such familiar terms you have placed yourself in the position of a sibling, only brothers and sisters may refer to each other in this way.'

She saw something flash across his face and wondered how she'd managed to anger him this time. It wasn't anger she'd seen there, but something far more dangerous.

He stretched across the desk, enveloping her hands in his. He turned them over and began to trace gentle patterns with his thumbs on her palms. Her insides melted and she forgot what she'd been about to say. She knew she should snatch her hands back, jump to her feet in protest, but an odd lassitude overtook her, and she left them where they were. Her head felt heavy, her neck too slender to support it; an unusual heat was pooling in her nether regions.

She jerked and this time extricated herself from his grip. 'Lord Colebrook, I must protest. You have no right to treat me disrespectfully. We are not betrothed.' No sooner had she spoken than she regretted it.

His expression triumphant, he was on his feet towering above her, eyes blazing. Next, as if she weighed nothing, he grasped the arms of her chair and swung it round so that her feet were facing outwards, away from the desk. Then, to her horror, he dropped to one knee and took her hands again.

'Exactly so, sweetheart.' His voice was low and intimate, sending shivers of apprehension, or perhaps excitement, up and down her spine. 'You must know how I feel about you. I've waited years to meet the right woman, and finally I have.' He paused and, raising her hand, delicately kissed each fingertip, his breath warm, the sensation like nothing she had ever experienced.

'Would you do me the inestimable honour, my darling girl, of becoming my countess? We can unite the two branches of the family, and our fortunes, and run the estates together.'

Unite their fortune? Is that what this nonsense was about? Keeping the money safely in the family? Her spurt of anger gave her the courage she needed to refuse his ridiculous proposal. This time she removed her hands with grace. She bowed her head, acknowledging his question.

'Lord Colebrook, kindly get up from the floor, you're making a cake of yourself. I have no intention of marrying you, not now or later. What a ridiculous idea! Why we're scarcely acquainted; and you've already tried to kill me *and* taken liberties with my person. I can assure you, I did not enjoy either experience.'

Now she *had* offended him. He was back on his feet, scowling down at her as if she was a recalcitrant member of his brigade.

'Very well, I shall accept your refusal for the moment. But be very sure, Miss Frobisher, the matter's not decided. Before you leave here you might be glad to have the protection of my name.' He spun and marched out, parade-ground stiff, every inch a soldier.

She didn't stop shaking for several minutes. Eventually she felt strong enough to stumble across the room and, believing she needed a hot drink, she tugged the bell-strap. She thought she might be ready for a bowl of soup as well; it seemed a long time since she had broken her fast that morning.

She waited fifteen minutes but no one came to answer her summons. How odd! She decided to go to the kitchen and see for herself what was keeping the maid. She pulled her shawl tightly around her before braving the icy corridor, and walked briskly until she reached the warmth of the grand hall. Here she paused in front of the fire glad the two tree trunks were still alight. Taking a deep breath she hurried towards the rear of the house and into the kitchen knowing it would be warm in there. She pushed open the door, stopping abruptly. The room was warm, the range burning, but of Cook and her two assistants there was no sign.

What was it about Neddingfield that one moment people were there and the next minute had vanished? She went out into the corridor that led to the boot room and saw there were no cloaks and clogs hanging up. Everyone had gone outside, but why would they do this when there was so much snow? She hurried back to the kitchen, went across and peered through the window. The blizzard had abated; the sky was clearing.

She would go and see Birdie; she would know what was going on. Hester picked up a candle, lighting it with a taper pushed into the range, then took the stairs that led to the house-keeper's domain. On opening the door the sound of sobbing was clearly audible, and the murmur of her companion's voice attempting to offer comfort. Whatever was going on?

The door banged shut behind her and the noise ceased; she heard footsteps and Birdie was there, her face etched with concern and, crouched on a chair beside the fire, first wringing her hands and then wiping her eyes on her creased apron, was Polly.

'Hester, my dear girl, I'm so glad you've come. I couldn't leave to fetch you, and it would seem there's no one else down-stairs to run errands. You'd better come in at once, and hear of the fresh disaster that has overtaken us.'

Hester went to Polly's side and squeezed her shaking shoulder. 'Whatever's wrong? Why are you so distressed?'

The girl gulped, shook her head, then made a valiant effort to answer. 'Oh, miss, it's dreadful. They've gone you know, everybody's left. I went to the kitchen as you requested, but it was empty. I checked the pantries, and the root cellar, but there was no one. I ran upstairs to our rooms in the attic and they're all empty too; Cook, the kitchen-maids, parlour-maids, everyone but Meg, have vanished into thin air, just like Miss Culley and my poor Sam and the rest of them.' The girl was overcome by another wave of weeping and buried her face in her apron once more.

Hester straightened, moving to join her friend by the window. 'Why have the staff left so suddenly? Are you certain that Meg's still here?'

'According to Polly she's sewing in your dressing-room. I haven't been up to look, but she was there an hour since, and unless one of the other girls went up to get her, she's there still.'

'I shall go at once and fetch her. It will be better if we're all together.'

She raced back down the stairs, across the passageway and into the back stairs to arrive opposite her chambers breathless and her candle flickering wildly. She blew the flame out before rushing across the passage and into her rooms.

'Meg, Meg, are you there?'

She heard a welcome noise and the girl appeared in the doorway. 'Here I am, Miss Frobisher, I was wondering what had happened to Polly, she's been gone that long. I was becoming a mite worried.'

'Meg, she's with Miss Bird. I want you to come with me. Leave whatever you're doing, and we'll go straight there together.' Having blown out her single candle, and not wanting to stop and fiddle with the tinderbox, she decided to take the long way round, which was bright enough in daytime.

All had disappeared – did that mean Ralph had gone as well? She froze and the girl running behind, unable to stop, crashed in to her. Hester fell to her knees, banging her elbow painfully on the wall. Meg was instantly overcome with apologies.

'I'm that sorry, miss, I didn't know you was going to stop. I do beg your pardon, I didn't mean to …

'It's not your fault, Meg. Kindly give me your arm and help me up.' She scarcely managed to form the words, to sound normal, and not alarm the girl further. She prayed that whatever had happened to the women, God grant the men, and especially Ralph, were still somewhere on the premises.

Ralph paused in the grand hall. He wanted to go outside and hit someone; he'd rarely been so angry. What was the matter with the chit? Couldn't she see he was offering her everything? He was an earl, wealthy, and in good health. Why had she turned him down so comprehensively?

He had to get out; he felt as if the walls were closing in on him. He took the stairs three at a time and charged into his apartment. Although Robin was officially his valet, since this nonsense had started he had reverted to being his second-in-command and was fully occupied elsewhere.

Miss Bird had arranged for a girl to take care of his clothes, rooms and personal needs. He had intended to shout for her, but he'd not yet discovered her name. For some reason she always scuttled about like a terrified mouse on his appearance.

It was immediately apparent that his chambers were empty. The door to the bedchamber was open and both fires almost burnt out. He nodded, presumably she'd run down to fetch more fuel. Then he noticed the coal bucket and the log basket were half full. He frowned. Where was the wretched girl?

He wasn't going to wait around. He was too impatient. He found his heavy coat, beaver hat, and gloves. Ramming his arms in he buttoned it up quickly. Then, with his hat and gloves in one hand, he headed out. As he passed the dwindling fires he paused. It wouldn't do any good to let them go out, as the girl would have to rake out the ashes and start again and his rooms would become cold. He threw his hat and gloves on to a side table and, grabbing the coal bucket, hurled the contents on to the fires. He then added several logs to each. Satisfied that both would burn for several hours without attention, he snatched back his belongings and ran downstairs.

He decided to leave by the front door. Slamming back the heavy bolts would allow him to spend some of his pent-up fury. He would like to go back into the study shake some sense into Hester. His mouth twitched. No, what he wanted to do was kiss her senseless, bury his face in her shining hair, make love to her until she could refuse him nothing.

The last bolt slid back and, turning the handle, he pulled the door open expecting to be deluged with an icy drift that had built up against the door during the blizzard. But one of the men had cleared the front steps, and the way down to the turning circle was free of snow. He glanced up at the sky; the snow had stopped, the clouds were moving away. The sun would be out soon.

He walked round the house pausing to admire the group of snowmen they'd built. He had believed they had reached an understanding, that she returned his regard, how could he have got matters so wrong?

The snow had blown across the gravel drive and piled up against the trees that edged it. He would walk to the gates and back, get some much-needed fresh air and exercise, and not have to struggle through snow up to his knees in order to do so. He would also investigate the matter of the floating lights Hester had mentioned. It had to be smugglers, and no doubt he'd see evidence of ponies or donkeys on the path when he looked.

He'd walked almost a mile when he spotted a break in the snowdrifts; there was a gap in the trees and the snow had funnelled through. This was the place he needed. He stopped, swearing volubly. That girl had addled his brains: any evidence of free-traders would have been obliterated by the morning's blizzard, so there was little point in him going to look.

He turned and begun to stride steadily back towards the hall. The sun came out as he'd predicted, bathing the ancient building in yellow light, making its dozens of windows sparkle; it looked attractive and not at all like a place where people disappeared mysteriously.

Not ready to go back inside, he walked round to the stables; he would check how the sick horse was doing. Hester's man Tom had worked wonders; it was a valuable beast and it looked as though, against all odds, it might recover.

The cobbled yard was strangely quiet, and he couldn't hear the women in the kitchen. Surely they should be preparing the midday meal of soup and pasties by now? The wooden doors of the stable block were shut tight, as one would expect. He pulled one open and stepped inside. Twenty horses munched contentedly in their stalls; the place warm and redolent of dung, hay and horseflesh.

At the far end he could see two men completing their duties clearing the last of the stalls. They saw him watching and touched their caps politely. He couldn't see Robin, Tom or any of the other men. They had to be about somewhere, perhaps these two would know.

He strolled the length of the building, pausing occasionally to pull a silky ear or stroke a velvety nose. He reached the far end where the men, one wielding the shovel the other pushing the wheelbarrow were waiting.

'Where are my men? In fact, where's everyone else?'

Ralph recognized the taller of the two men as the one who'd volunteered to accompany him earlier. 'I don't rightly know, me lord. We've been busy 'ere. I reckon they could be in the tack-room. I've not seen them for an hour or more.'

Ralph nodded his thanks and headed back to the centre of the building, turned down through the narrow passage that led to the half-a-dozen storage rooms. He could hear the sound of raised voices. Pushing open the door he found Tom and Robin arguing and both turned guiltily at his entrance. Robin, who had been speaking, faltered to a halt.

'What's going on here? Where's everybody else?'

The men exchanged glances, but it wasn't Robin who replied, but Tom Clark.

'It's like this, my lord, they've gone. All the women, and all but two of the men. They collected their belongings and left as soon as the snow stopped.'

Ralph stared from one to the other. 'For God's sake, why? They've got a soft billet here, good food, comfortable quarters and generous remuneration. What could have possessed them to walk out in weather like this?'

Again it was Tom who answered. 'Ghosts, sir. First Miss Culley and the rest disappear, then the gates were barred with no one here to do it. Then, the two men who tried to capture Polly – remember one of them vanished into thin air? I didn't think much about it at the time, but I did wonder where he'd gone.'

Ralph was beginning to understand. 'Are you telling me that that they've left because they believe Neddingfield Hall is possessed by evil spirits or some such thing?'

'I am, my lord. Last night several of the men saw lights floating in the woods, winking on and off, and heard ghostly moaning and clanking. James disappearing without trace was too much. They decided they'd rather be home, and hungry, than here with spirits and the like.'

Ralph looked at Robin. 'And you? How do you feel about all this? I don't hear you denying the existence of the supernatural.'

He saw his man flush, and for the first time since he'd known him, Robin failed to meet his eyes. 'Generally, I don't believe in this sort of thing, my lord. But now, I'm not so sure.'

Chapter Twelve

RALPH TURNED HIS back in disgust, how could this most reliable of men be having doubts at such a crucial time? Ghosts had nothing to do with what was happening here, humankind must be behind it.

'Good God! Don't be a fool, Robin. Don't let what's happening unnerve you; I need you strong, beside me.'

He heard shuffling feet and then received a light tap on his arm. He glanced over his shoulder, but it was Clark standing there not Robin, *he* had left the room.

'You can't blame him, my lord. What's been going on up here isn't natural, and he was with you when you went to look for young James; he told us how there was no evidence anywhere of other horses or anyone else who could have spirited him away.'

'Then why are you here, Tom Clark? Do you not support the theory that we're being haunted?'

'Whatever I believe's no matter, sir. I'd lay down my life for Miss Frobisher any day, and ghosts, witches – whatever it might be – I'm staying put until the … until the matter's resolved.'

'Good man. Will Robin leave?'

Tom laughed. 'Leave? Not likely! He'll not leave. He's mighty afraid of what's going on, but he'll stay to the end like me. Your old coachman, Fred, went with the others, but to try and persuade them to return. He'll be back and stay put with us.'

'I doubt the last two men from town will feel the same way.' Then he knew Robin had gone to try and persuade them to stay.

'They must move into the house; we have to remain together. I shall close down the main part of the Hall and everyone must use the servant's quarters.'

With only a handful of staff it would be impossible to keep the Hall warm anyway. The matter decided, he went to look for Robin and the two remaining men; he could hear them talking amongst the stalls. To his surprise both the men greeted him with a grin.

'Take more than a few spooks to send us packing, me lord. We'll stay; between us we can take care of these nags for you. We'll not need to move into the 'ouse; we'll sleep down 'ere with the 'orses.'

'I shall double your wages, of course. I insist that you move into the house, all of you. I want to know where everybody is at all times.'

The two men exchanged looks and nodded. 'We'll be getting our belongings and come across right away. The fire will 'ave to be doused. We'll bring Fred's things as well, shall we, my lord? This lot are done; if the snow clears we can turn the farm 'orses out.'

Now that Meg, Polly, Birdie and herself were all safely established in the kitchen, Hester felt more sanguine. There was no sound from the yard, but the stables were too far away to be able to hear anything from there. Some of the men remained and she was sure that Ralph would not have deserted her. He was a soldier, he'd not leave his post.

'I see that Cook has prepared the vegetables for the soup, so all we need to do is put on the pot and cook it. Even I can manage that. Meg, could you see how much bread we have in the pantry?'

Polly went with her, the two having decided that as long as they were staying they would not leave each other's side. Hester couldn't blame them – she was determined to stay close to Birdie.

Her cheeks coloured as she thought there was someone who would be only too happy to hold her. She suppressed a smile, knowing being held by Ralph would be more dangerous than remaining on her own. What had recently passed between them must be put to one side. She was prepared to do so and prayed that he would have forgotten his anger at her rebuff.

The soup was bubbling on the range, fresh pasties warm from the oven when she heard the unmistakable sound of the back door opening. All four women froze. Then she relaxed.

'It's Lord Colebrook and some others coming in. Thank God, we're not entirely alone.'

Ralph appeared in the doorway, behind him Tom, Robin, his coachman, and two stable hands carrying their bundles. His smile made her knees weaken.

'I see you know what's happened, sweetheart. Miss Bird, can you find accommodation for the outside men? Give them the rooms the women vacated.'

My goodness! Not only had he forgiven her he was larding his remarks with endearments and she was not the only one to notice this.

Birdie, who had been kneading the next batch of bread, raised her eyebrows before wiping her hands on her apron. 'Of course, my lord. Miss Frobisher has already suggested *we* move in together.'

Hester watched her friend hurry away and heard her talking to the men outside; the sound of heavy boots on the backstairs echoing round the kitchen as they were taken up to their new quarters.

Gesturing to Ralph that they walk to the end of the kitchen, away from the others standing around the range warming themselves, she said, 'We can't manage this house with only five men and two girls. I think we should all eat in here as well as sleeping in the servants' wing.'

He nodded. 'My thoughts exactly. At least this way we can keep warm.' Raising his hand and tenderly brushing away the lock of hair that had escaped from its place, he said nothing; he didn't need to, his expression said it all.

After lunch they began the process of moving belongings. The outside men took off their boots and joined in, happy to carry and fetch as required. By the time it was dark, everything had been arranged to Hester's satisfaction.

'I don't know what we shall eat this evening, Birdie; you know I'm not skilled in the culinary arts.'

Her friend smiled. 'I have thought of that, my dear. I shall take over the role of cook. My repertoire is limited, but I can make bread, pastry, soup, and roast meat reasonably well. Between us I'm sure we shall not starve.'

'It will be strange eating with the staff, and I'm sure they will find it as uncomfortable as I shall.' Hester continued to polish the silver cutlery as she spoke, laying it out on the scrubbed oak table neatly.

'Good heavens! My dear girl, we shall not eat together, and the staff shall certainly not use the best cutlery.'

'Then how shall we arrange it?'

'Lord Colebrook and yourself shall dine first; I intend to spread a cloth on this table, and bring in the silver candlesticks from the dining-room. When you've finished you retire to the new sitting-room upstairs and then the rest of us shall eat.'

'I don't think it's right that you have to eat with the servants – you're my friend.' Hester saw that Birdie was about to protest and forestalled her. 'It's all right, I understand. The staff need you to keep them cheerful.' She stared across to the window. 'It gets dark so early. I'll not feel safe until all the shutters are closed, the hangings pulled and the doors locked and bolted. Once everybody is inside perhaps I can relax.'

'The men are out settling the horses and milking the cows. Lord Colebrook told us they would be back before it was fully dark. You must try not to worry, my dear, or you will come down with one of your megrims.'

'At least we don't have to dress for dinner anymore. We should look ridiculous in our silk finery sitting at the kitchen table.'

'I shall make it look more formal, my dear, never fret.'

The noise of the men returning interrupted their conversation. Hester removed herself upstairs and left the kitchen to Ralph and the other men. She wasn't sure how she would react to spending so much time alone with a man who, in spite of her initial reservations, she was now beginning to find irresistible.

It was a strange experience sitting opposite Ralph in the kitchen, sparkling crystal and the best silver laid on the white cloth as though they were eating in the grand dining-room, with the heavy warmth of her dog's head across her feet. Jet was now sleeping inside as everyone knew he was as good as any man if it came to a fight.

Meg and Polly were serving dinner; Birdie had retired to the servants' hall and was organizing the table for when the staff ate later on.

'Ralph, do you think the horses will be safe out there?' She was concerned about Thunder.

'I don't see why not, we know these people have their own nags, although God knows where they are, so why should they want to take ours? Nobody's going anywhere at the moment, there's too much snow.'

'That's another thing; it puzzles me that all this has happened as though planned. How could anyone have known we would be snowed in?' She saw his expression change and a wariness in his eyes, an uncertainty she hadn't seen before. She swallowed her mouthful and it stuck somewhere in her chest. She knew why he looked that way. No one could possibly have known it was going to snow unless they were not … not of this world.

She dropped her cutlery on the plate. Polly and Meg were standing by the scullery door, out of earshot, but in the quiet of the kitchen the dropped silverware on porcelain was unmistakable.

Hester lost her appetite. She knew she couldn't force another morsel down however tasty. She mustn't let her fear show; it was her duty to maintain a brave face; somehow she forced her head up and bit her lips to stop them trembling.

'I'm feeling unwell, my lord. I fear I might have eaten something that disagrees with me. Pray excuse me.' Hester pushed back her chair and, clasping a napkin to her mouth, hurried out but forgot to pick up a candlestick to light her way.

The corridor was warmer than before; Ralph had ordered the fires at either end be set, and the wall sconces flickered brightly. She could hear the murmur of voices further down, and knew that everyone was safe inside. She was halfway across the corridor when an arm encircled her waist.

'Sweetheart, what's wrong? You've eaten nothing the rest of us haven't had so what has upset you?'

Hester felt her resistance draining away. Why should she fight this attraction? There was evil stalking them. She could feel it gathering around her, and they might both be spirited away by tomorrow. She didn't want to meet her Maker still unsure what being a woman really meant.

She stepped closer, into the warmth of his embrace, resting her cheek against his shoulder, inhaling his familiar scent. He needed no further encouragement and his arms closed tight about her and for the first time since she'd arrived at

Neddingfield Hall she felt secure. They stood entwined for a moment and then common sense reasserted itself and she pushed gently at his chest and was released immediately.

She left one hand there as she looked up. 'We need to talk, Ralph, but here is not the place. We might be living cheek by jowl with our staff, but some things are still best kept private, don't you agree?'

His eyes burned into hers and she felt his heart thundering beneath her spread fingers. 'Wait here, sweetheart, we need a candle. We shall break our necks if we try to climb the stairs without one.'

He returned and with his arm around her shoulders guided her up, holding a single candle aloft to light the way. She hardly registered the journey, her head was full of images of forbidden pleasures. Her mama had told her what took place between a man and woman in the marriage bed, had told her that it was a duty she would have to endure, and Hester had always thought that this side of matrimony would not be to her liking.

Indeed, she realized, as they reached their destination, it was her knowledge of the vastly unpleasant activities involved in becoming a wife that had added to her determination never to marry. But when she was with Ralph she became confused. She wanted to know what it would be like to run her fingers through his thick hair, feel his lips on hers, have him caress her.

Ralph continued to urge her in the direction of his parlour, but some instinct made her pause. 'I think, my lord, it would be best if we remained here. This is to be our sitting-room in future. See, there are two day-beds and several armchairs around the fire; we shall be quite comfortable.'

She slipped out of his loose grasp and walked purposefully towards a small curved armchair. If she sat in that she would be safe – there was room within its arms for only one. As she reached the rug that had been spread across the scrubbed boards, he was beside her, blocking her path.

'Shall we sit on the *chaise-longue*, my dear? It's nearer to the fire and away from the draught of the door.'

She hesitated a moment too long and before she could refuse she was being guided to the piece of furniture he'd indicated. She had no option, and unless she made an unseemly fuss, she must sit with him.

Smoothing her skirts, she settled gracefully, crossing her ankles demurely and placing her hands in her lap. She kept her eyes lowered, finding his piercing stare unnerving. He sat down next to her, but kept a seemly distance, leaving almost two feet between them. Her pulse began to slow, wild thoughts of wantonness dispersed; she was once more in control of the situation.

'Do you intend to leave the shutters closed in the main part of the house, or open them each morning to give the impression we are living as usual?'

He didn't answer, stretching out his legs, crossing his ankles and staring at the toes of his polished boots as if he suspected they had sprung a leak. She waited for a moment, believing he hadn't heard her polite enquiry and prepared to repeat it. 'My lord, I asked if you …' The words dried in her mouth as his head swung towards her and she saw the predatory gleam in his eyes.

He was playing games with her, had sat so far away in order to spring his trap when she least expected it. She sprang to her feet, believing she could escape into the safety of her bedchamber. She was too slow. Before she had time to take a step he was beside her, his bulk obstructing the path, solid as a wall.

It had been her intention to pass by, asking him icily to step aside. But he didn't touch her, didn't speak, just stood there, inches away, waiting for her to move. She felt a strange heat spiralling from her toes to her breasts. She had stood as close to gentlemen before, but all she'd been aware of was their body odour, the smell of alcohol or tobacco on their persons, never had she wanted to close the gap.

She swayed and, as she did so, his arms grasped her and her feet left the floor as he lifted her until she was on a level with him. All thoughts of protest evaporated under the heat they were generating. Her hands inched upwards, over his chest, until they reached the strong column of his neck. Her thumbs paused under his jaw, feeling the pounding of his pulse and knowing she was the cause, filled her with elation.

This released the last of her inhibitions and, forgetting all she had been told about the dangers of allowing a gentleman to take liberties with her person, she buried her fingers in his hair, tilting her head to give him access to her lips.

Her eyes fluttered shut as his mouth burned an imprint on hers; at first the pressure was gentle, his lips firm on hers, but then she was crushed closer, felt something hard pressing into her stomach. Her lips softened and he deepened the kiss; his tongue slid along her lips sending waves of pleasure around her.

She strained closer, wanting something more, not certain exactly what. With something resembling a groan he twisted his long body back on to the *chaise-longue* bringing her down with him so that she lay trapped by his weight against the high padded back.

Her head was whirling; he removed his mouth and began to trail soft, hot kisses down her cheek, her jaw, and lower still until he was kissing the curve of her breasts. The bodice of her gown felt too tight, in fact all her clothes were constricting; she longed to remove them and feel her flesh and his meld together. He was pushing down the shoulder of her gown, continuing his exploration, and she thought she'd go mad from the heat that burned inside her.

Suddenly the stair door crashed back and a hundredweight of

jealous canine launched himself across the room, teeth bared, a terrifying growl rumbling in his throat. In one smooth movement Ralph was on his feet and standing behind the day-bed, breathing heavily and backing away from the dog.

Hester felt the hot wet tongue of her pet on her nakedness and the heat of passion evaporated. 'Get off, you stupid dog. Get down. Let me adjust my clothing.' She heard a door further along the hall slam shut. Ralph had retreated to his bedchamber; she wasn't sure if she was angry or relieved by Jet's sudden intervention.

However, as her head cleared she realized they both owed the animal a debt of gratitude. They had been making love in public; anyone could have come upstairs and caught them; her good name would have been besmirched and Ralph's honour gone; even marriage would not have removed the stain.

Such things were only supposed to go on between married couples and then only in the privacy of their bedchamber. It was as though an icy pail of snow had been poured over her head. Shamed by her wanton behaviour, she scrambled to her feet and ran to the bedchamber she was sharing with Birdie.

Jet flopped down outside the bedroom door, content that he'd done his duty and saved his beloved mistress from disgrace.

Chapter Thirteen

HESTER LAY STILL, staring up at the sloping ceiling, unable to think where she was. Then there was a flicker of candle-light and she knew.

'Birdie, is that you?'

A soft chuckle greeted her comment. 'It is indeed, my dear, who might you be expecting at one o'clock in the morning?'

'Goodnight, Birdie, I'll talk to you tomorrow.'

An hour passed and she tried to suppress her overwhelming desire to empty her bladder. Eventually she accepted the inevitable. She would have to get up and find a commode if she wished to sleep any more that night. She knew there was one placed discreetly behind a lacquer screen in the far corner of the room, but she couldn't bear the thought of using that with Birdie in the other bed. No, she would have to venture outside her bedchamber and find somewhere else.

She slipped out, pushing her feet into slippers and, taking her robe in one hand, crept towards the door. There was sufficient light from the glowing embers in the fireplace for her to see her way. She pulled open the door and hesitated.

Her toes bumped the recumbent form of her dog stretched out like a hearthrug across the door. It was a good thing she hadn't stepped straight out or she'd have tripped over him and roused the entire household. Pulling the door behind her, she waited for her eyes to adjust to the darkness.

The large grate on the far side of the room had been replenished with coal and she crossed to the fire. Removing a candlestick from the mantelshelf she lit it from the embers.

Jet, happy to have company, padded after her, nosing her thigh, making a low rumble of greeting in his throat. 'Shush, silly boy. I can hear you. I have to go downstairs. I suppose you'll come with me, and I shall be grateful of the company.' Hester knew the best place to look for relief would be in the main part of the house. It would mean first finding her way in to the freezing grand hall, and then to a small anteroom in which she was certain there was a commode.

Descending the stairs was no problem, and she was glad the dog was close beside her, as the nearer she got to the bottom, and the further away from the others, the more nervous she felt. Remembering what had happened the last time she'd emerged unexpectedly from similar stairs she stopped, pushed on the door and sent her pet ahead.

He bounded through and stood, head to one side, tail wagging, waiting for her to join him. The passage wasn't cold, but she knew venturing in to the main part of the house would be decidedly unpleasant.

On impulse she slipped along to the boot room and removed a cloak and slipped her feet into the nearest pair of clogs. Her candle flickered and wavered on the shelf as she tied the ribbon at the neck and pulled the hood over her head. The dog watched her with growing excitement.

'No, I'm not going outside, not in the middle of the night. You'll just have to wait until the morning.' She reached down and stroked his head. 'I suppose if you must you'll find a corner somewhere.'

Picking up her candlestick she walked along the passage to

the door that led into a main thoroughfare. On pushing it open an icy gust of wind tore past her, extinguishing her candle. Paralysed by fear she flattened herself against the wall believing she was in the presence of an evil spirit. What else would create such a blast when all the shutters and windows were closed?

She clenched her jaw to stop her teeth from clattering. Then a cold nose pressed impatiently into her hand and her breath hissed through her teeth. 'I'm being ridiculous, aren't I? If there was anything supernatural in the house you would be the first to detect it.' Reassured by the dog, she gathered her wits trying to visualize how far it was to the grand hall where she might be able to relight her candle. Her mouth curved a little, she already had the perfect guide.

'Come along, old fellow, you lead me to the hall.' She twisted her fingers in to his ruff and pressed close to his side. He seemed to understand and immediately moved forward. She kept at his side, letting him take her along the inky corridor to where she would find what she so desperately needed.

After a few minutes she thought she saw a flicker of light ahead – good, the fire must still be burning, the tree trunks alight. She shivered as another icy draught swirled around her feet. She was pleased she'd had the forethought to add an extra layer to her night clothes; it was freezing on this side of the house and her face was unpleasantly chilled.

They were almost into the hall when she stopped. It was too cold – there could be no fire burning here. Her skin prickled. If the fire was out, what was the light she had seen?

She whispered to her dog, 'Jet, do you think it safe? You're not growling, your hackles are down, so have I nothing to worry about?' The dog nudged her, and the sudden movement almost made her lose control of her bladder. She had to find a commode, she would worry about the light afterwards.

Not pausing to light a candle, just using her excellent sense of direction, she turned towards the door and, with one hand trailing across the panelled walls, continued round the hall until she came to the door she needed. 'Wait here, Jet, I'll only be a moment.'

Inside it was so dark, it was worse than being in the stairwell. She recalled that there was a tinderbox and candlestick inside the door. Could she manage to do this by touch alone? Eventually she created a spark and the fluff burnt brightly, long enough for her to relight her candle. She lit a second candle and placed her own next to the commode.

Her clothing readjusted, comfortable at last, forgetting about the icy blasts and the strange light, she stepped out of the anteroom, remembering to snuff out the spare candle. She expected her dog to be waiting, but he wasn't there. The single candle failed to illuminate the area and as there was no red glow coming from the massive grate she only had a single flame to guide her back.

'Jet. Jet, where are you? Come here, boy.' Her voice sounded loud in the emptiness. There was no response. Should she call again? Leaning against the wooden walls her candlestick flickered in the darkness.

Would it be sensible to wait for Jet? Suddenly the sound of the dog barking as if he was trapped inside the very walls echoed around the deserted hall. Grabbing her skirts she fled, her mind racing, wild thoughts of ghosts and hobgoblins uppermost. Her beloved dog had been taken this time and trapped forever in the fabric of the building. Hot tears trickled down her frozen cheeks, but she ignored them, just wanting to reach Ralph and the sanctuary of his arms.

The frantic tapping on his door dragged Ralph from a fitful slumber in which he had been chasing his love through the mist and no matter how fast he ran she always remained out of his grasp.

'Ralph, Ralph, let me in, please let me in. Jet has been taken. The ghosts have got him.'

Christ in his Heaven! What disaster had occurred this time? In one fluid movement he rolled out of bed and, in his underwear, threw open the door. Hester fell into his arms.

'What is it, sweetheart? You're shaking. Come in quickly before you wake everyone.'

Leaving the door fully open, his wits having not quite forsaken him, he gathered her near, loving the feel of her wet face on his naked chest. He stroked her back, murmuring soothing nonsense to her until she calmed.

'Ralph! You've no clothes on.'

'And you, my love, have on far too many.' His passion-fuelled brain cleared as the significance of her garments registered. 'Why are you in clogs and a cloak? Good God! You've not been outside?'

She wriggled free and stepped across to stand in front of the fire. 'Of course not. I went downstairs to … Well I needed to go into the hall and Jet came with me.' Her voice faltered and he saw fresh tears in her eyes. 'He's vanished, Ralph. The ghosts took him. One minute he was there the next I could hear him barking in the walls. He's been spirited into the fabric of the house to bark and growl for eternity.'

If she hadn't looked so wretched he would have laughed at her nonsense. 'I'm sure there's a rational explanation, my love. Sit by the fire whilst I make myself presentable, then you can explain exactly what happened.'

He pulled on his britches and shirt, hastily pushing in the tail, then grabbed his boots and rammed his bare feet straight in. He smiled grimly – the last time he'd had to dress in such a hurry had been in Spain when his brigade had come under attack from a bunch of renegade Frenchies.

Decent, he turned back to face the young woman who had been watching his every move with obvious interest. He felt a second surge of desire but forced it down. There would be plenty of time when things returned to normal.

'Tell me, darling girl, what frightened you?'

'I already told you, I went downstairs and Jet vanished, only his ghostly barking left behind.'

He attempted to hide his smile, but she was not pleased by his levity.

'Sometimes, Colebrook, I wish I'd never made your acquaintance. It's no laughing matter; my dog's gone and all you can do is snigger.' She tossed her head and her eyes flashed.

In two strides he was beside her. Forgetting the reason she was there, he lifted her into his arms and closed her mouth with his. For an instant she resisted, then she melted against him and he was lost. Her gentle pressure on his chest forced him to release her.

'Ralph, you cannot keep doing this. There are more important matters for us to attend to.' She gazed at him, her lovely face flushed with passion and he ached to consummate their love, forget the danger and lose himself in her. She saw his expression change and understood.

'No, Ralph, this is neither the time nor the place. I shall wait outside for you.' Wisely not remaining to hear his response she stalked out giving him vital minutes for his passion to subside. He doused his face in cold water from the jug on the night stand and pulled on his top-coat. The makeshift sitting-room was ablaze with candles, she had not been idle these past minutes.

'Hester, I must beg your forgiveness, yet again, for—'

She raised her hand. 'I'm as much to blame as you. Now I'm here, safe with you ...' Her lips twitched as she said this and he felt his groin responding. 'I think I might have overreacted and there must be a sensible explanation, although I cannot think what it might be.'

'Go back to bed, sweetheart. I'll wake the rest of the men and we'll search downstairs. You shall come to no harm whilst I'm here, I promise you.'

'Next time, perhaps you'll overcome your scruples and use the facilities in here,' Miss Bird said wryly, as Hester climbed back in bed.

'I know, it was foolish of me, but I didn't want to wake you. Jet has been stolen away and it's my fault.' She blew out the candle and pulled the comforter over her head hoping her companion would offer no comment.

'Whatever you might think, my dear, however much the evidence points to the contrary, I'm still not convinced that these mysterious disappearances have anything to do with the super-natural. Think about it, no one has actually *seen* a ghostly presence; there have been no white shapes floating in the air, no moaning and clanking of chains, have there?'

'No, I suppose not. But my dog has vanished and I heard him barking, but he couldn't get to me.'

The bed creaked as Birdie settled down again. 'But it's far more likely that he's got himself shut into a cupboard. Don't fret, my dear, Colebrook will discover him, if not tonight, then tomorrow when it's light.'

In sombre mood Hester accompanied her friend downstairs at dawn next morning. The two girls were also unusually quiet. Perhaps the missing dog was upsetting them too. No one had had much sleep and all were ready to start at the slightest sound.

'Meg, get the range burning and I'll make us a hot drink. Polly, finish off the bread and get it into the oven as soon as it's hot enough.'

'What shall I do, Birdie? It's too dark to go outside and I don't wish to stand around idle whilst everyone else is busy.'

'If you must do something, my dear, take the candle down to

the root cellar and fill up the basket with a selection of vegetables for today's meals.'

Hester wanted to refuse, having no wish to go into the dark on her own after all that had happened. Knowing this was irrational, she was not entirely convinced their problems were caused by anything mortal. She sighed. Everyone else was busy – there was no choice, all must do their part today.

The stone steps to the cellar were cold and she wished she'd thought to put on clogs for her indoor shoes had thin soles that were not suitable for this task. The cellar was icy – the bitter wind spiralling through a gap in the external trapdoors. Placing her candle on the shelf she unhooked the basket from its nail and began to rummage amongst the vegetables. The pile was mountainous and in the feeble flickering light it was hard to tell a potato from a mangel-wurzel whatever that might be. The sooner this unpleasant job was over, the quicker she could return.

She heard steps on the ceiling; she would recognize Ralph anywhere. Putting the heavy basket over one arm, she lifted her skirts and, candle in the other hand, she hurried up the stairs. She emerged into the scullery and left the vegetables on the table. Her hands were thick with mud and she turned back in search of a pail of water to wash them, but there was none; no one had been outside to fetch fresh water.

She found a clean rag and did her best to remove the soil from her hands. She could hear Ralph talking to Birdie and then she heard the bolts being drawn back in the passageway that ran parallel to the kitchen. He was going out, and he hadn't bothered to come in and bid her good morning. After what had passed between them, they were more than good friends, surely?

Rushing into the kitchen, she skidded to a halt in surprise. 'My lord, I thought I heard you going out.'

She watched his mouth quirk. Hastily she pushed her hands

behind her back. 'I know, there's no water and we all have to do our bit since we have so few staff here.'

'I know, sweetheart. It's not your hands I was concerned about – you have a large smudge of dirt across your cheek.'

Mortified she clapped her hands to her face adding to the mess. 'Don't you dare to laugh at me. If you were a gentleman you would not stand there smirking, but find me something to remove it.' Her words were sharp but her eyes were laughing.

He reached into his coat pocket and, removing a clean white handkerchief, pointed to a chair. 'Sit down, my dear, and I shall restore your countenance. At the moment you look like an urchin.'

Hester saw him tip a small quantity of hot water from the kettle warming on the range, on to the cloth. She noticed his fingers were strong and brown, not like the white hands one associated with the aristocracy. She settled comfortably on the upright kitchen chair and tilted her face.

He squatted in front of her, then reached out and, grasping her chin, briskly rubbed away the mud. His touch was impersonal; he didn't take the opportunity to stroke her face lovingly and there was no sign of the warmth and passion they had shared the previous night. She felt herself shrivel inside. Had her wanton behaviour given him a disgust of her? Was she considered a girl with no morals, someone unsuitable? She tried to twist her head from his hand, but his fingers tightened.

'Sit still, you goose, you don't want anyone else to see you like this, do you?'

Even his voice was matter-of-fact, like an exasperated parent, not a lover. It was too much. She hadn't wanted to fall in love with him, not wished … her head flew back. She couldn't help the gasp of pain as her already tender skull cracked painfully against the wooden chair. Tears filled her eyes that had nothing to do with distress.

'What is it? You ninny, let me look.'

His sympathy was too much for her frayed nerves. A surge of anger at him, at the loss of her beloved dog, at everything, raged through her. 'Remove your hands from my person, Colebrook. Haven't you done me enough damage already? I'm quite capable of taking care of myself. Why don't you go and do something useful? Find my dog, for instance.' Her icy glare was returned in full measure. She saw him swallow and his lips thinned. He straightened, glowering at her.

'I beg your pardon, Miss Frobisher. I have no wish to intrude.'

She knew he was very angry. Should she apologize, tell him it was her headache that had make her speak so, but she couldn't find the words and he turned his back, the matter unresolved.

The clatter of cutlery heralded the arrival of Birdie, but when he greeted her companion his manner was friendly, his tone light. Whilst they were conversing about the events of the night, she slipped away, across the passageway back upstairs to her bedroom where she found a facecloth to complete what he had started.

She wasn't going to go downstairs until she was certain he was outside; she had no wish to see that look in his eyes a second time. She busied herself tidying, as the girls were helping in the kitchen and the dairy and had no free time to come upstairs.

She made up the fire, cleaned out the ashes, and dusted the room. Pleased with her efforts, she washed her hands again, brushed her skirts free of dust and was done. She looked around; there was nothing more to do. She would sit on the window seat and read her novel.

She stared out of the tiny casement and gasped. Neddingfield *was* haunted – they *were* dealing with ghosts. Only the supernatural could have enabled the snowmen to move themselves across the grass and turn to face the woods. She had to speak to Ralph; it no longer mattered if he was cross with her, she needed him, as he was the only one who could protect her from the evil that was closing in.

Chapter Fourteen

RALPH HEARD HESTER leave and cursed himself for mishandling the situation. He had deliberately adopted a more formal manner, believing she would not want to be reminded of what had almost taken place the night before. He knew being forced to live in such close proximity was going to become a test of his inner strength. His lips curved as he remembered her softness, the way her eyes looked in to his with such sincerity....

'My lord, what do you think?'

He had heard nothing Miss Bird had said in the past few minutes; he had been woolgathering. He nodded sagely and said something ambiguous hoping his answer would satisfy whatever question she had asked previously.

'I shall leave you to continue your excellent management of the house, Miss Bird. I must go outside and search for the missing dog.' Robin was waiting for him looking even more disconsolate than he had yesterday.

'My lord, I think we should leave this place, not stay until we've all been picked off one by one. Neddingfield is haunted.'

'Nonsense. Someone is trying to convince us the place has ghosts; it's up to you and I to disprove it. Good God! You've faced far worse. Don't waver now, Robin, I need you by my side.'

'I'm not leaving you, I didn't say I'd do that. What I'm saying, sir, is that we should all go before it's too late. Polly was here a moment ago telling Tom those snowmen you built have walked across the park. I tell you that's not the work of humans. I never met walking snowmen, not even in Spain.'

'God's teeth! What next? Are you coming with me, or are you going to hide in here?'

Robin scowled, but tied his muffler tighter. The sky was heavy, no sign of the sun today.

'I think we're in for more snow any minute, Robin. Even if we wanted to leave, by the time we're ready, there'll be a blizzard blowing.'

Checking his pistol was in his pocket, he led his reluctant valet outside to investigate. Sure enough the snowmen were no longer in front of the study window, but had moved fifty yards nearer to the wood and were facing in the opposite direction. There were no footprints in the snow, and the smoothness behind each could be interpreted as the pathway they'd made as they shuffled forward of their own volition. In spite of his reassurances to Robin he felt the hairs on the back of his neck prickle.

Ralph walked up to the first snowmen and pushed it; it shot forward several inches as if on wheels. 'Good Lord! So that's how they did it. Here, Robin, help me tip this object upside down.' As he'd expected, the base was sheet ice, so his theory was correct. 'Ingenious, but no ghosts involved. Somebody sliced this from its base, then tipped water over it and waited until it froze. It would have been easy to slide them along the grass and leave them as they are now. They couldn't have done it if the snowmen hadn't been solid; remember, the past twenty-four hours it hasn't risen above freezing.'

He watched Robin walk over to the other snowmen and found they had all been treated in the same way, saw the tension draining from his man and knew finally all thought of ghosts had been dispelled. 'Whoever is orchestrating these events has been helped by the unseasonable weather. No doubt if there had

been no snow we would have been treated to floating appari-
tions and clanking chains.'

'I'm sorry, my lord, but until this moment I was almost sure
there were ghosts here. But if this is man-made then so were the
rest of the events. Which means that dog must be somewhere.'

'Birdie, do you know where Lord Colebrook is? I need to speak
to him most urgently. Do you know the snowmen have moved?'

Meg, who had been setting out the requirements for luncheon
dropped the cutlery she was holding with a clatter on the floor.
'Oh, Miss Frobisher, Polly and I saw them last night. We quite
made up our minds to leave today, but once it was light and we
were all down here together, things don't seem quite so scary.'

'What nonsense is this? The snowmen moving? I rather think
not. Just forget about it and get on with your work, my girl.'

Meg curtsied and knelt to pick up the spilt knives and forks.
'Yes, madam. I'm sorry, I'm sure.'

Hester was about to continue the conversation when her
companion shook her head. 'Why don't you put on your cloak
and go and see how the horses are doing? They haven't been
exercised for two days so no doubt they'll all be in need of
company and distraction.'

'I shall do that, Birdie. Where's Polly? I've not seen her this
morning.'

'She's gone with Smith to show him how to milk a cow; no
doubt they'll be back here in due course.'

It took barely ten minutes to change into her stoutest boots,
put on her pelisse, warm cloak and bonnet. She paused, glancing
into the small mantel mirror to check her appearance. In spite of
her lack of sleep her eyes were sparkling and her cheeks becom-
ingly pink. Being in love obviously suited her.

It was strange how these things happened, but she supposed
that she and Ralph had spent more time together in the past few

days than many couples did in six months. She knew as a fact that her dear friend Charlotte had only spoken alone to her prospective husband on three occasions before he made her an offer. They had both known they would suit from the first moment, Charlotte had told her firmly. She frowned. It was a great shame their initial delight in each other's company had so quickly faded. If they had known each other longer, would they still have married?

She scowled. She had no intention of giving up her freedom, the fact that she found herself inexplicably in love with Ralph didn't mean they had to become man and wife. No, even if he did propose again, and she accepted, she would insist on a long engagement. He could come and spend some time with her at Draycot Manor and she would attend soirées and musical evenings in London with him during the season. Maybe such pastimes would be pleasant if escorted by someone like him.

Outside she felt a few flakes of fresh snow dampen her upturned face; they were already knee deep in the wretched stuff, and the last thing they wanted was any more. She comforted herself with the thought that if they were unable to move then the same should apply to those who wished them harm. Birdie was right: it was ridiculous to think that the Hall should suddenly be inhabited by a host of ghosts at exactly the same time that her aunt disappeared and Ralph inherited an unlooked-for peerage.

In spite of the shortage of manpower the cobbled pathways were swept clear and her journey round to the stable block was accomplished without mishap. She paused as she passed the dairy; she could hear Polly's voice as she explained how you churned the cream into butter.

It was fortuitous that the girl had turned out skilled in so many tasks. Hester felt ashamed of herself, she was several years the girl's senior, but she had spent her life in idle luxury. Without Birdie and Polly none of them would have eaten and the cows would have gone unmilked.

As she reached the stable doors she saw Ralph and his valet approaching. She was about to call out a greeting when she saw a familiar shape hurtle from the woods and the words froze in her throat.

'Jet! Jet, where have you been, you bad dog? We have been so worried about you.' The animal's thick coat was snow encrusted, but otherwise he appeared unharmed. He threw himself at her and reeling backwards, unable to keep her balance on the slippery stones, she tumbled sideways into a snowdrift, her dog on top of her.

Thinking this was some new kind of game, instead of allowing her to stand, the wolfhound put his paws on her chest, pinning her to the ground, and covered her face with wet licks.

'Get off! Stop this nonsense.' Ralph's voice snapped like a whip and the dog obeyed instantly. Hester lay dazed, unable to move, three-quarters of her person smothered in snow. 'Up you come, my love.'

She found herself yanked unceremoniously to her feet. Before she could protest, he started to bang her clothes with such vigour she almost tumbled anew.

'Stop it, Ralph. I'm quite capable of removing the snow for myself.'

He grinned up at her from where he was crouching at her feet vigorously shaking snow from the folds of her cloak. 'There, I've done now. Where did the animal come from? He shot past us so fast, I didn't have time to look.'

'He came from the path that leads into the woods, but how he ended up there I've no idea.'

'Neither have I. Go inside, darling, I'll deal with this.' He grinned down at her and a delightful warmth spread through her insides. 'Robin, find Tom and bring him indoors with you. We'll need lanterns if you can find them.' She hesitated, not wishing to leave his side. 'Sweetheart, although I've removed the worst, as the snow melts you'll become chilled.' His expression was serious as he continued, 'There's a lot more coming, and we can't send for help. Whatever's going to happen here we shall have to deal with ourselves.'

Putting his arm around her waist he hurried her along the path making it impossible for her to speak, as she needed all her concentration to maintain her balance. Ralph threw open the back door and they both stepped in just as the snow began, obliterating the pathway in seconds.

'Here, let me help you take off your cloak and bonnet.'

She'd been about to tell him she was quite capable of doing it herself, but saved her breath. She fingered her pelisse; apart from the cuffs and hem it was dry.

'It's so cold, I think I'll keep this on. Ralph, tell me how you think Jet came to be in the woods when the last time I saw him he was in the hall?'

'You said that you heard him barking after he vanished?'

'Of course! I said he sounded as though he was inside the walls. He must have found a secret passage, though how he managed to open something like that on his own ...' Her voice faded as she realized the only way her dog could have entered a secret passage was if someone had left it open.

'I told you, sweetheart, whilst there's breath in my body no one shall harm you. This does mean someone tried to get in last night. Your dog's a bloody marvel! Without his intervention you could have been taken.'

She wasn't sure if she was more shocked by the suggestion that she could have been abducted, or by his language. 'Ralph! Such profanity is not something I'm used to hearing.'

He reached out and grasped her arm, pulling her towards him. 'I'm a rough soldier, my love. You'll have to get used to hearing the odd curse or blasphemy.'

He continued to draw her inextricably nearer. They were

standing in full view of everyone. Flustered, she settled on her heels, throwing her weight back. His mouth curved; instead of exerting more pressure, he did the reverse. Taking a stride forward, thus unbalancing her, she found herself falling towards the floor. He was able to catch her before she reached it.

'Let me go, Ralph. I have no wish to be manhandled in this way.'

To her astonishment he released his grip and let her drop the remaining few inches with a thud. Incensed, she glared up at him standing astride her prostrate form, thick brown hair in disarray, like a pirate in a storybook.

Neither of them heard Miss Bird emerging from the kitchen to see what all the fuss was. 'My dear girl, you have a nasty propensity lately for tumbling to the floor. Kindly stand aside, Lord Colebrook, and allow me to assist Miss Frobisher to her feet.'

He stepped to one side, his lips pressed together trying not to laugh. She was in no mind to do so. 'Thank you, Birdie, I should be grateful for your assistance as none has been forthcoming elsewhere.' She sent a dagger look in his direction, but he winked at her roguishly then turned away to greet Robin and Tom as they clattered through the door.

Their appearance gave her the impetus to bounce upright bristling with annoyance. Adopting her most formal tone she addressed the back of his shaking shoulders. 'And another thing, Lord Colebrook, kindly desist from larding your conversation with unnecessary and unwanted endearments. It's neither appropriate nor helpful.'

Not waiting to hear his response, Birdie's scandalized stare was enough to tell her she should have kept the comments to herself; she skipped nimbly into the kitchen, placing herself firmly on the far side of the table, waiting to see if he followed her in.

Chapter Fifteen

HOW COULD SHE! She had no decorum. Even someone as little versed in etiquette as he was aware that such remarks should not be made in front of the servants. He glanced up to see both men trying hard not to smile. He frowned and they sobered.

'Good, get those lanterns lit, Clark, and we'll go secret passage hunting. As we're certain there is one it shouldn't be too hard to locate.' He patted his pocket and nodded at Robin. His man answered immediately.

'Yes, my lord, we're both armed. Neither of us go far nowadays without a pistol in our pockets.'

As Tom fiddled with the lanterns, the back door shook; this was followed by a fuselage of barks. Ralph smiled. 'I believe we've left the most crucial element of our search outside. If the dog remembers where he went, maybe he can lead us back there.'

He marched up and down the endless passageways pressing and knocking, rubbing and banging every protuberance, every knot hole, but found nothing. 'We've spent the best part of two hours searching, even the dog has given up and gone back to the kitchen. I suggest we do the same.'

His two henchmen followed him back to the rear of the house; they went to the servants' hall, he to the kitchen. He wasn't sure what his reception would be from his volatile sweetheart, but he knew they would enjoy a lively exchange of opinions.

'The snow must be another yard deeper, Birdie. I doubt if the grooms will be able to attend the horses this evening.' Hester hadn't heard the door open, but was aware that Ralph was in the room. She called to him, but didn't turn. 'Ralph, what will happen to the livestock this evening?'

He spoke from beside her. 'The cows will be milked before it gets dark and the horses have enough fodder and water to last until tomorrow.' He lowered his voice before continuing, 'Are we friends again, darling?'

'Of course we are.' She glanced up and wished she hadn't. Her heart somersaulted and the familiar wave of heat enveloped her. He didn't need to speak, his expression told her he felt the same.

'Miss Frobisher, your dog is sitting in the scullery looking pitiful. I reckon he's after food.'

Relieved to be interrupted, she stepped round Ralph and smiled at Polly. 'I'm sure he is. I shall come and attend to his needs immediately. One cannot let a hero remain unfed.'

She spent the afternoon with Birdie; they played a round or two of piquet and then wrote letters to friends. Hester wondered if they would ever be delivered. They were to eat an informal supper, cold cuts and pickles followed by apple pie and cream.

'I think it best if you join Ralph and me this evening, then the staff can spend the evening in the hall. Do you agree?'

'I do indeed, my dear. As you know, initially I was delighted that you and Lord Colebrook would be obliged to spend time in each other's company, however it would seem that your relationship is developing at an alarming rate. I think it would be best if I chaperoned you until this … until this matter is resolved.'

'I appear to have fallen in love with him. My affections have been engaged so swiftly, but we spend most of the time at daggers drawn.'

'It's as plain as the nose on my face, my dear, that he's head over heels in love with you. I can't believe it – you shall be a countess by and by.'

Hester tossed her book to one side. 'I said I had feelings for him, not that I intend to marry him.' She laughed at her friend's disbelieving look. 'We're scarcely acquainted. I shall eventually agree to his proposal, but even then our nuptials shall not take place for a year at least.'

Birdie snorted but made no further remark. Jet, who had spent the afternoon lounging in front of the fire stood up and looked hopefully towards his mistress.

'Very well, I'll let you out. It's not quite dark so I expect the men are still outside to take care of you.'

'I shall come down and supervise the evening meal. Those two girls are excellent workers, but, like you, spend far too much time in the company of the male servants. I understood that Polly was betrothed to someone who worked here – if that's the case then Tom is going to be disappointed.'

Hester had also noticed a growing attachment between her man of affairs and her new maid. 'I don't believe anything official has been said. According to Polly they were merely walking out together. I think Tom will make an excellent replacement.'

'That was delicious, Miss Bird. You're a woman of many talents and without your skills we would have been on short commons indeed.'

'Thank you, my lord. If you wish to drink tea I shall go down and make it later on.'

'I've been thinking, Ralph, although we haven't yet discovered any secret entrances, we know there must be one. If we lock all the internal doors will it make us safer?'

He stood up and came round to pull out her chair. 'I've already done so, my love. However, I think your dog is the best deterrent we have. No one is going to get upstairs without him alerting us. I suggest, ladies, that you sleep in your clothes tonight.'

Hester swallowed. This suggestion was not because of the inclement weather. 'I thought that we could play a hand or two of whist, but I warn you, Miss Bird is an excellent card player.'

The next two hours sped past and it was after nine o'clock when they were disturbed by the sound of running footsteps on the staircase leading to the sitting-room. She stiffened and Ralph was on his feet and moving towards the door before it opened.

Polly, closely followed by Meg, burst in. 'Oh, my lord, they've gone. Seth and Robert went half an hour ago to check the doors and make up the fires in the passageway and they've not returned. Tom sent us up here to ask if you could come down, my lord, and please to bring the dog with you.'

Hester was on her feet to guide the distressed girls on to the day-bed. 'Sit down by the fire. We shall be quite safe up here together whilst his lordship finds the men.'

Ralph gestured with his head that she join him by the door. 'Here, sweetheart, take this pistol and keep it close. I want all of you to go into your bedchamber and bar the door. Don't open it unless it is me outside.'

'Take care.' She blinked back her tears, not wanting him to go with such an image of her.

Ignoring the three interested spectators he stepped closer and her arms encircled his neck as his closed around her waist. She tilted her face to receive his kiss knowing it might be the last time she saw him.

Tom and Robin were waiting at the bottom of the stairs, lanterns lit and pistols ready. 'How long is it since you saw the men?'

'About half an hour, my lord, Tom and I were playing cards and didn't notice the time. It was Polly told us they hadn't returned.'

'I take it you've searched the house?'

Both men nodded. 'And the doors were locked, the keys still hidden in the table drawer in the kitchen, my lord.'

'Good. At least that narrows our search. The entrance must be in the grand hall or along one of the corridors that leads up to it. It can't be this side of the house or we'd have heard them.' He looked down at the dog. 'It's up to you now, old fellow. You must find the entrance to the passageway, or the next time they come in here might well prove fatal to your mistress and me.'

Ralph extracted his own pistol, checking it was primed and ready to fire, then took the lantern Tom was holding. The only way forward was to find where these bastards were coming from and take the fight to them. The way things were, his assailants were having it all their own way, picking them off one by one.

'We'll start in the grand hall. Tom, you go to the left with the dog, and Robin to the right with me.' They had searched meticulously once before, but this time the scent would be fresh and with luck the dog would pick it up.

It was black as pitch. His breath steamed in front of him, swirling around the yellow glow of the lantern. He was relieved that both men knew they were not tackling the supernatural, it was enough to make anyone nervous. He was about to start his search when he recalled something Hester had said about her unpleasant experience the previous night.

'No, it can't be in here either. Miss Frobisher said she could hear the dog barking a distance away; if he'd found the entrance in the hall she would have seen it herself and he would have sounded nearer.'

He stood for a moment. 'What we're looking for will be in the main passageway that runs between the drawing-room and dining-room. As before, you take the left, Tom.'

He searched the area thoroughly but found nothing – taking the dog with them this time had proved of no assistance. Ralph had no option – he had to find it or they could all be dead by morning.

Halfway down the passage he began checking the wall in which the doors to the various rooms were situated on his own, whilst the other two and Jet continued on the far side. They had no luck, everything was as it appeared, no panel swung inwards, no rosette of carved oak turned under his probing fingers.

A deep rumbling alerted him; the dog had metamorphosed into that terrifying beast. He crossed the corridor to join Tom, Robin close behind him. He whispered to his companions, 'It's here, the dog can smell them.'

Jet, his hackles up, was growling softly, as he sniffed the panelling. He stopped and pressed his nose against an innocuous panel as if expecting it to swing inwards. It didn't. The animal continued to vibrate like distant thunder.

Without a word being spoken the three men started a painstaking search of what appeared to be wood like all the rest. The dog sat, as if waiting for them to open it. Ralph gestured to the others to stand back and raise their lanterns and he did the same. He was missing something. He raised his lantern higher and from his superior height immediately saw what he wanted.

'God's teeth! It's here, right in front of our eyes, and we missed it because we were looking on the wall and not the ceiling.' Pointing upwards, he stepped across and reached out to press what looked like a knot hole in the black ceiling beam. The depression in the wood was worn smooth, as if by constant rubbing, whereas the rest of the wood was rough to the finger-tips.

There was a faint hiss, a barely audible click, and a section of wall swung inwards. The dog bounded in. Ralph leapt forward, grabbing him. 'Quiet, Jet, we don't want to warn them we're coming, do we?' He gave the dog a small shake and the noise ceased. He blew out the candle inside the lantern and the others did likewise; the flickering of their lights might warn whoever it was of their coming. There were a dozen, at least, and their only hope of success was surprise.

He kept his hand firmly in the dog's fur, believing that Jet would lead him, as he had done Hester. He turned to the two men behind him. He couldn't see them, but could hear them breathing heavily.

'Robin, take hold of the tail of my coat. Tom, take Robin's. That way we'll stay together; the dog can guide us.'

Jet padded forward, his hackles stiff, his nose to the ground, following a recent scent. Ralph hoped that one of the men had had the sense to bring a lantern and tinderbox, as they might well need one later on. The passageway descended steeply and the stone walls he had been feeling under his fingertips gave way to earth. They were outside the house now – God knows how much further to go.

They'd been travelling sometime when he felt the dog tense and almost imperceptibly the growl began again. He knew they must be near their destination. He flattened himself against the side of the narrow passage and, pistol cocked and releasing his hold on Jet, he waited, straining his eyes and ears, hoping to get a clue as to what might be facing them.

He didn't know what the dog had sensed; it was as dark and silent as a grave ahead. He reached down, but the animal had gone, slipped away into the darkness. Buggeration! They were totally blind now. Keeping his fingers on the wall, he crept on, his men following behind. But something had changed. What was it? His mouth curved. It didn't smell as rank and the air was fresher. The passageway was widening; there must be a chamber ahead.

He stepped forward and his hand was floating free, no wall beside him. Before he could warn the others there was a faint scuffle and he was seized from behind, his feet kicked out from under him, and his head enveloped in a stinking sack. His pistol fell uselessly to the ground and he had only his booted feet as weapons. As ropes were tied round his writhing body he used these to good effect and landed several punishing blows on the shins of his assailants.

The satisfying crunch of boot on flesh elicited no cries of pain, no swearing, no reaction of any sort. If he had not known he was dealing with flesh and blood he would have been truly terrified. Two men grabbed his heels and he was hauled some distance, his head cracking on the ground, and then tossed roughly against a wall. For a moment he was dazed.

Robin and Tom were being given similar treatment and the thuds as they fell beside him echoed eerily. There was a faint glimmer of light filtering through the filthy material, but not enough to distinguish anything. Rough hands rolled him over and, feigning unconsciousness, he was thrown backwards a second time. There was the faint shuffle of footsteps as the men departed and then impenetrable darkness and thick silence.

Where was the dog? Why hadn't he attacked? There was nothing to do until his hands were free. He lay still. Had the men with the lantern left? Alert to every sound, it became apparent there were more than just Robin, Tom and himself held captive. Was it possible James and the two grooms were also here unhurt?

Although he was tightly trussed, his fingers were able to reach down to his boot top in which he'd slid a stiletto knife he'd liberated whilst in Spain. Grasping the hilt he pulled it out and began the laborious process of sawing against the ropes that held him fast.

At last his hands and arms were free and, snatching the noisome sacking from his person, gratefully drew in air that wasn't tainted. Edging forward on his knees until his questing fingers touched a shrouded shape he slashed through the ropes that bound this man, certain from the shape and smell that it was Tom.

'Is that you, my lord? If you give me the knife, I'll release the rest of them. Do you know how many we're up against?'

'No, I'm going to reconnoitre. When everyone's free, quarter the area and see if you can find the pistols. Do it by touch alone, don't light the lantern or make a sound.'

Leaving him to release the others, he dropped to his stomach and shuffled forward on his elbows, uncomfortable but effective, as it kept him below the eyeline of anyone who might be watching.

His eyes became accustomed to the darkness; there was a faint glimmer ahead so there must be a lantern burning. He continued his painful progress until close enough to see there was a group of eight or nine men standing around a brazier conversing in sibilant whispers. He squashed himself against the wall and strained his ears. What he heard made his blood run cold. These men had mistaken him for a servant and he thanked his Maker fervently that he was dressed in his oldest clothes and so still breathing: the bastards were now going back to the Hall to murder Hester and himself.

He'd began to reverse slowly when, to his horror, the men moved. Rolling sideways, his face and body pressed into the earth, he prayed he would remain unnoticed as they hurried past.

Would his own men be ready to attack, or would they lie, pretending to be constrained, until the others had passed? His life hung in the balance and he didn't even have his knife to protect himself.

The first three men went past, their lanterns held aloft, leaving the ground in darkness. They must have been, by his calculation, almost up to the side chamber in which his men were hiding, when suddenly there was the sound of a ghostly howling. Two men who were parallel with Ralph crashed into the men in front.

'Bloody hell! It's that noise again. I'm beginning to think this bleeding place really is 'aunted.'

The leader of the gang snarled, 'Shut your trap, Jones; it's that bitch's dog, I'll slit its throat when I get my bleedin' 'ands on it. I reckon one of you stupid bastards left that panel unlocked again.'

The men fell silent and resumed their progress and Ralph knew he was safe – for the moment. He waited until he was sure he couldn't be heard by the two guards or the raiding party, then sprang to his feet, racing to join his men.

'Robin, you keep Seth and Robert with you and deal with the guards; they'll not be expecting an attack. James, I am damn glad to see you alive and well after your incarceration. You and Tom, come with me. We have to stop them before they reach Miss Frobisher and the other women.'

Chapter Sixteen

HESTER SAT WITH her arm around Polly whilst Birdie comforted Meg. She knew she should try and say something uplifting; it was her place as their mistress, but all she could think of was Ralph risking his life to save them all.

'How long have they been gone, do you think?'

'I heard the clock strike nine just after they left and it hasn't struck again, so it's less than an hour, my dear.'

'I'm not sure we should have locked ourselves in your parlour, we have no commode in here.' Too late she realized it was a mistake to draw attention to their lack of facilities. She felt Polly shift uncomfortably beside her, and knew she needed to relieve herself. 'I think that it should be safe enough for the two girls to go into your bedchamber, if they lock the door behind them.'

'Very well, if the need's urgent, I can see no harm in it.' Her companion stood up and ushered them to the door. 'I shall unbar this, and wait until I hear you lock yourselves in the bedchamber. Do you understand what you have to do?'

Hester saw the girls nod, too frightened to speak. Polly had her arm around her friend; she was obviously the more courageous of the two. 'When you're done, knock on the wall, and we can let you back in here.' She supposed it would have been more appropriate if they had used the commode first, but their need at the moment was not desperate.

Ten minutes later the wall reverberated, such was the ferocity of the banging coming from the bedchamber. 'Birdie, I'll stand behind our door whilst you collect them.'

She was poised in the half-open doorway when she heard her dog barking somewhere downstairs. He sounded frantic; even from this distance she could hear his paws scrabbling on the wood. Without stopping to think, she left her post and raced downstairs. If Jet had returned alone something catastrophic had occurred. Her dog would not have deserted Ralph unless he'd good reason to do so.

The animal didn't pause to receive her petting but tore up the stairs and vanished into the temporary sitting-room. She gathered her skirts and prepared to run after him. The wall sconces made the stairwell bright as day and it would be obvious where they were if she left them burning. She blew out each one as she ascended, hoping they would have cooled and the distinctive aroma have dispersed before their enemy arrived.

'Miss Frobisher, your dog's gone right past us; I think he's scratching at the attic doors,' Polly told her.

'Quickly, take your shawls and come with me. Jet wants us to follow him; something terrible's happened and we need to hide. Close the doors to both the rooms. Be quick! We haven't a second to lose.'

Knowing the lives of the others depended on her courage and intelligence she led them forward, pushing her despair aside. If they could find somewhere in the depths of the attics to hide it would give them time and Ralph might still return to save them.

'Bring candles and a tinderbox, girls.' Birdie grabbed Meg's arm and half dragged her towards the staircase that led up to the attics. Hester was glad Polly needed no second bidding; the girl snatched up two candlesticks and rammed the tinderbox in to her apron pocket before joining the others at the stairwell.

'All right, Jet, we're coming.' She opened the door and the

dog padded ahead of them, calmer now they were following him. Holding her candle in front, Hester tried to see where the animal wished them to go. He worked his way through piles of debris, old chests, broken chairs and a miscellany of unwanted items.

She stopped and looked around. 'Look, Miss Bird, take the girls and go behind that row of trunks. If you crouch down I'm certain you will be invisible.' They didn't argue, just hurried over and she watched them vanish into the gloom.

'Excellent. I can't see you, I'm going to hide with Jet. Whatever happens, whatever you hear or see, don't come out of hiding until … well, until it's safe.'

The only thing that might reveal the whereabouts of the other three were the footsteps they'd left in the dust. She removed her cashmere wrap and, bunching it up in one hand, swept away all evidence of their passage. Her dog began to growl, his hackles rising and she knew she had to hide herself or be discovered.

Hester could feel her dog quivering with anger, knew that someone was coming who didn't wish her well. Suddenly there was a hideous moaning and the sound of clanking chains. Her hair stood on end and an icy shiver ran up and down her spine. Only Jet's weight pressing against her side prevented her from crying out.

He was poised beside her, ready to pounce. She wondered what the other three were thinking as the hideous noise drew nearer. The sound of heavy footsteps coming up the stairs reverberated round the attic; after each footfall there was an ominous thump as if something heavy was being dragged behind. She buried her face in Jet's fur and prayed for deliverance.

Ralph, lantern swaying wildly in front of him tore back along the underground passageway until he reached the secret entrance that led into the Hall, relieved it had been left open. He hadn't found his pistol so headed for the gun-room. There was no point in racing upstairs until they were armed.

This side of the building was quiet, the men from the cellar had to be somewhere in the house, but noise coming from the servants' quarters could not be heard here. Not bothering to keep his passage silent he crashed into the room and stopped.

Where the bloody hell were the keys? There was no time to waste searching, as they needed the weapons: it was imperative the cupboard was opened immediately. Putting his lantern down on a shelf he looked around the room for something to use as a lever to break open the cabinets. 'Tom, James, find something to prise the lock.'

'Here, my lord, this should do it.' James threw over a heavy iron file, one which was used by a smith to pare down a horse's hoof. Whilst they gripped the edge of the door he forced it into the crack, and threw his weight against it. The door sprang open. Snatching out the pistols, he tossed two to Tom, one to James, keeping the last two for himself.

'Take powder and shot; quickly, they have been here too long already. Load your pistols – have them primed and ready to fire.' Whilst they were still fumbling, he removed a sword and belt from the rear of the cupboard and strapped it around his waist.

'Remember, we have the advantage of surprise, but there are seven of them. Be ready to fire at any moment. Keep the lanterns low, and hold them behind you whenever we approach an entrance.'

He ran back, but as he reached the corridor leading to the rear of the building, he slowed. It was a while since he'd wielded a blade, but feared his pistols might not be enough.

He walked soft-footed across to the first staircase, still unable to hear evidence of an attack ahead of him. Keeping his shoulder to the wall, he arrived at the head of the stairs and paused to listen again. Nothing. Beckoning the other two, they also slid into the makeshift sitting-room. In the light from his lantern it was clear the four doors were open, both parlours and bedchambers empty. Ralph thanked God that Jet had arrived in time; Hester had taken everyone to hide somewhere safer.

'The attics. They must be up there,' he mouthed.

With lanterns at floor level he moved down the corridor to the second staircase, freezing, as a hideous moaning echoed from the stairwell followed by the sound of chains clanking on the ground. Despite the certain knowledge that they were dealing with mortal men his stomach clenched and icy sweat broke out on his forehead.

'Bloody hell! What's that?' Tom whispered.

'I know what it sounds like, but remember these men have set themselves out to frighten us; to convince us we're being attacked by supernatural forces. What better than clanking chains and ghostly moaning to terrify us into submission?'

'And they're doing a bloody good job of it, my lord. I hate to think what the ladies will make of it.'

Ralph surmised there was barely a minute to position himself and his men before the women were discovered.

'Make sure your pistols are cocked, and shoot to kill. Don't give anyone a second chance.'

He heard James's sharp intake of breath, and knew the lad thought his orders harsh – after all hadn't these same men captured him and left him alive? But neither James nor Tom had heard what he had; he knew all this masquerading was merely a means of reaching Hester and himself in order to dispose of them. He would not let that happen.

Removing his pistols from his belt he handed his lantern back to Tom, gesturing for both men to stand behind the door, as he wanted no light to filter on to the stairs and warn the bastards. He was calm; his pulse steady; his mind clear. He was a soldier and this was a battle he didn't intend to lose.

Pausing at the door, he tried to guess where his opponents were. As he hesitated, there was a canine roar of rage and a man screamed in agony. This was his chance. They would be distracted. Bursting into the stairwell he found he was behind a group of men who blocked the exit, all rooted to the spot. The frightful noise of the dog savaging one of their comrades in the darkness had them petrified.

He raised his gun and shot the nearest man; the sound announced his presence as nothing else could. A second man turned, levelling his own pistol, but Ralph was too quick for him and his second pistol exploded. The man fell dead, tumbling head over heels towards him. Ralph swung himself over the body and it tumbled harmlessly to the bottom. Not waiting to see if his men were ready to fight, he erupted into the attic prepared to dispose of the rest, single-handedly if necessary.

Hester knew the men were close, the clanking and banging had stopped, but she was sure there was someone breathing a few yards from her hiding place. She gripped her pistol more firmly, clicking back the pin so the gun was ready to fire. The noise sounded loud in the darkness and she prayed it had not revealed her hiding place.

This slight movement seemed to tell her dog it was his turn to act. With a snarl of rage he launched himself over the top of the trunk hitting the first man squarely in the chest. She heard the man screaming and then the darkness was rent by cursing and shouting. This was her opportunity.

Peering above the barrier and in the faint light cast by a lantern on the floorboards, she could see that there were several men already in the attic. It was only a matter of time before they were all taken. She had to protect the others. Raising her gun she pointed it at the man who was belabouring her dog with a club, trying to dislodge him from his death grip on his comrade's throat. Then there was a hideous sound of gunshots.

One, then another, and she added to the cacophony by pulling *her* trigger. Her aim was true and the man with the club fell with a grunt to the floor. He lay across the body of the man he'd been trying to protect. She thought it wise to remain where she was, behind the trunk; she'd done her part, it was up to Ralph to do his. He was here, the gunshots from the stairwell told her so.

Ralph saw the dog tearing the throat from one man and another raining blows on the dog's head and shoulders with a cudgel. He leapt forward, drawing his sword. Before he could intervene Hester appeared from behind a row of trunks and, pointing her pistol, pulled the trigger.

He dropped to the ground as a further fusillade of shots ricocheted around the attics, the smoke from the guns making it impossible to tell friend from foe as his enemies were firing indiscriminately. He gestured to her to stay put; she nodded, vanishing once more. Her dog remained on guard, growling, warning anyone against approaching.

'Tom, James, to me.' He rolled to one side as a shape loomed above him. Raising his sword he stabbed upwards and felt the blade sliding into solid flesh. The man he'd cut staggered away, groaning horribly. How many more of them were alive? Where the hell were Tom and James? In the mêlée the lantern had been kicked over and plunged them all into darkness.

Tom's reply came from the direction of the stairs. 'We've killed one of the bastards, sir. James is shot, but he'll live. I'll stand guard; no one will come down without me seeing them. I have three pistols loaded and waiting.'

The remaining men registered the import of Tom's words. They were trapped. All Ralph had to do was keep them away from the ladies; if they took one of them hostage he would have to surrender and all would be lost.

He had excellent night vision and crouched in the darkness waiting for his eyes to adjust. Tom's lantern sent just enough light spilling from the doorway to make it possible to see. Seven men had passed him when he had been hiding in the underground passageway. He'd killed two, Hester and the dog had disposed of another two, Tom and James one more each which meant there was one man left in the attic.

Yes! He could see him edging slowly towards the stairwell; Tom and James would be an easy target, the lantern showing up their outlines. He couldn't allow this last man to reach them. In one fluid movement he was on his feet, sword raised. The man collapsed with a crash as the sword pierced his heart.

Ralph straightened, looking round for the man he'd sliced earlier. He saw a fourth body and shrugged. It was over. The seven men were dead. It was a pity the injured one hadn't survived long enough to be questioned. He'd let the militia sort that out when the weather cleared and he could send another message to fetch them.

He heard muffled sobs coming from behind another row of trunks and guessed it was where the other ladies were hidden. 'Tom, bring the lantern; we need to get the ladies away from all this mess.' He heard them shifting behind the trunk. 'I should stay where you are, Miss Bird, let me sort things out before you bring out the girls.'

'I understand, my lord. We shall remain where we are until you tell us to move.'

He saw the light approaching and headed towards it. 'How's the boy, Tom?'

'I'm shot in the shoulder, my lord, not about to meet my Maker.' James answered cheerfully. 'I can help you and Tom tidy up.'

'Excellent; don't overdo it – we have sufficient corpses already.' Ralph dropped his sword on the floor not wishing its bloodstained blade to be seen. 'Hester, sweetheart, you stay where you are as well. There are things that need doing before you come out.'

'I know. We're unharmed, thank God! I knew you'd come.'

He heard her swallow back a sob and wanted to go and take her in his arms. The thumps and bangs on the stairs indicated the corpses were being removed from there. There was just suffi-cient light for him to drag the bodies over and drop them on top of the two that had fallen by her hiding place.

He hoped in the darkness they might be invisible. There was nothing he could do about the congealing blood on the boards; he'd just have to guide the ladies past and hope they would be so concerned with finding their way in the gloom, that they wouldn't notice.

The dog was no longer growling and greeted him by banging his tail on the hollow side of the trunk. 'Well done, old fellow. You're a fearsome beast, but without your help this could have had a different ending.'

There was the sound of shuffling and his beloved spoke to him, her voice steady, her previous distress under control. 'I'm coming out. I refuse to crouch behind here a moment longer. I just killed a man, and watched my dog tear out the throat of another. It's far too late to consider my sensibilities.'

Holding out his hand to guide her she walked straight into his arms where she belonged. 'My God, you're shaking. Sweetheart, it's almost over. We can send for the militia tomorrow and let them find out who's behind all this.'

She didn't answer, pressing herself against him and, despite the circumstances, he felt the all-too-familiar tightening in his groin. He smoothed his hand up and down her spine and felt her relax against him.

'All clear down here, my lord. Shall I come up with lanterns? James is safely on the day-bed – he'll do for the moment.'

'Can you hang a lantern in the stairs, Tom? I don't think we need further illumination up here at the moment.'

The man understood. 'Very well, sir, I'll come up with both hands free.'

Ralph called to the others. 'You may come out now, Miss Bird. Take care where you walk. I suggest that you go straight down to the kitchen; it's warmest there, and you must be chilled after your sojourn up here.'

'Of course, Lord Colebrook. I believe that a restorative drink would be beneficial before we think of retiring tonight.'

Miss Bird was a treasure. Keeping his arm firmly in place he waited whilst this paragon escorted her two charges out from their hiding place.

Hester saw Tom arrive and hurry over to assist Birdie and the girls. The three women stumbled past the pile of corpses, apparently unaware of their presence, and vanished downstairs. She was content to remain where she was, loving the feeling of Ralph's arm around her, his strength slowly restore her equanimity.

Something Tom had said finally registered. James had been shot; he was wounded and still untended. She allowed herself to be guided down and out to the sitting area where Birdie was waiting, the girls had continued down to the kitchen. She saw James stretched out, his face ashen, jacket bloodsoaked, and forgot her own discomfort.

'James, lie still whilst I fetch my bag. We must stop the bleeding.'

'No, my dear girl, allow me to take care of James. You go downstairs; you have much to discuss with Lord Colebrook.'

'If you're sure, Birdie. If you need any assistance call me at once.'

'Come along, darling. Miss Bird is going to take care of James. He's lost a deal of blood, but the shot passed cleanly through his shoulder. He'll make a full recovery.'

Hester didn't argue; his words were to reassure her for he hadn't had time to examine James, neither had he spoken at any length to Tom about the young man's condition. The good Lord had taken care of them so far, she would leave the matter in His capable hands.

The kitchen was warm, the range still burning brightly, candles lit. She stopped, puzzled.

'How can this be? Who has been down here and opened the range and lit the candles?'

Ralph kissed the top of her head. 'Look, the candles are almost burnt out and the range no doubt the same. It was left like this when all the fuss started. My dear, Polly and the other girl must take care of you. Tom and I have to go back and assist Robin and the two grooms.'

She stared at him in bewilderment. 'I thought you said everything was over, that we're safe, and now you tell me you're leaving again.' She knew she sounded hysterical, but she couldn't bear to think of him going back into danger for a second time that night.

Chapter Seventeen

'SWEETHEART, I SHAN'T be gone more than an hour or so. I must be sure the last two villains are secure.' One of them had better be breathing so he could be interrogated. Her lips quivered and he almost changed his mind. 'Please, don't wait for my return; when you have had a hot drink, retire. We shall talk in the morning.'

She was going to protest, but he forestalled her. Stepping close, for the second time that night he embraced her in full view of the servants. She snuggled against him and, tightening his hold, forgetting the circle of interested spectators, he lifted her from her feet and covered her mouth with his. Never had he felt such passion; tomorrow, when things were settled, whatever the weather, Robin would ride to find the nearest vicar.

Reluctantly lifting his head, he whispered softly in her ear, 'I love you, and intend to marry you as soon as it can be arranged.' As she slid down his chest, her softness aroused him further. Her eyes told him his feelings were returned.

'I shall take hot water and drinks up to James and Birdie. Godspeed, my love, come back to me safely.'

Unable to reply he raised one hand, seeing too late that there were blood smears on it, and caressed her cheek. Unbothered by the gore she covered his hand with hers and smiled sweetly.

'My lord, shall we take the dog with us?' Tom spoke from behind him, sharply reminding him of his pressing responsibilities.

'No, he's done enough tonight. Jet can stay here and guard the ladies.'

The return journey down the passage was made at speed, the necessity for silence and secrecy gone. Both pistols were reloaded, but the sword still languished on the floorboards in the attic so the belt and scabbard had been discarded. The danger was over; Robin was an expert at springing an ambush and the guards would either be dead or captured by now.

There were lights ahead and Robin's voice called out, 'Thank God! I was about to come in search of you, my lord. We had no problems here; one dead – one ready to be questioned.'

Ralph felt a surge of excitement. The information he needed would be his before the night was out and tomorrow they would seek out the leader. None of the intruders was the man he sought; that person was well spoken, a gentleman, and these were no more than rough ex-soldiers.

'James received a bullet through the shoulder. However, there are seven cadavers to remove and I need Seth and Robert's assistance with this matter.'

He looked around the roughly circular space that had been hewn out of the ground, the walls supported by beams, the ceiling also. There was a ladder leading up to a trapdoor at the far end. The two men nodded and grinned at him. 'Well done; you shall not go unrewarded for this night's work.' Glancing at the bodies on the floor of the cave it was obvious that one was dead, the other securely tied, unconscious. 'Robin, you stay here. Tom, can you clean up at the Hall?'

'Where do you want me to put the bodies, my lord?'

'Outside. It's so cold they'll not turn putrid for a day or so. Pile them up in one of the outbuildings.' He walked over to stare up at the trapdoor above his head. 'Has anyone been up to discover exactly where this comes out?'

'That we have, sir, but there's so much snow you can't see a damn thing out there. We could be anywhere.' Robin nodded towards the pile of empty barrels piled against the far wall.

'It's a smuggler's den; somewhere they can hole up when the excise men are on their trail. From the looks of the walls this has been here a long time. Probably when the house was built the owners were involved in free-trade and had the passageway put in.'

Ralph was not so sure. 'It's more likely to have been a priest's hole and the smugglers took it over. At least we know now how they were able to vanish. But God knows how the bastards found out about the passageway or the way to release the mechanism.' He yawned. 'No doubt I shall discover the truth tomorrow.'

Deciding it would be easier to interrogate the prisoner in privacy, away from someone more squeamish than himself or Robin, he waited until the others had gone. 'Wake him up. The sooner I have the information I need the sooner I can get some shuteye.'

The kitchen seemed overlarge without Ralph. Hester turned to the girls who were waiting politely for instructions. 'Polly, is there any milk in the pantry? I think I would like a mug of choco-late with a large dose of medicinal brandy in it. Would you like the same?'

'That would be grand, miss. Meg and I can make the drink, but I wouldn't know where the brandy is kept.'

'Thank you, Polly. There's some in the study, I'll fetch it. I'm sure that both Miss Bird and James would appreciate some as well.' This time she was content to venture into the dark on her own. There was no need to worry about intruders; Ralph had dealt with them and she was safe.

The cognac was in the decanter exactly where she'd seen it last and triumphantly she returned to the kitchen. Polly had already found the milk and it was gently steaming in a copper saucepan on the range. Meg was busy assembling the necessities for tea. The girl looked up at her shyly.

'I thought that his lordship and the others might prefer a brew of tea, miss; the gentleman don't generally like chocolate.'

'Good idea; make a pot for James now, but leave everything ready for when the men return.' She realized that in spite of all the excitement of the evening she was ravenous. 'Meg, find the bread and butter and see if there's any of that ham left from supper. We shall make them all a midnight feast.'

Once she was certain they knew what to do she hurried upstairs to see whether she could be of any assistance to Birdie. James was sitting up, a neat bandage around his shoulder. He was a trifle pale, but apparently in good spirits.

'Good heavens! How are you feeling? There will be sustenance and tea arriving soon, but I have some brandy here for you both.' He looked uncomfortable at being discovered without his shirt on.

'Thank you, miss, I'm not too bad. Miss Bird has done a splendid job patching me up. She's gone to wash her hands and then she's going to find me something to wear.'

Hester tipped a generous measure into the crystal glass she'd removed from the pocket of her skirt. 'Here, drink this. I'm going to see Miss Bird.' Her friend was drying her hands when she entered and greeted her with her usual calm.

'There you are, my dear. I'm about to venture upstairs to find something for poor James to put on. I thought this blanket could go around his shoulders for the moment.'

'The girls will be bringing up chocolate and some cold cuts and bread and butter. I should like something to eat before I retire. Will James require any sutures?'

'I don't think so, my dear. The bullet had lodged near his shoulder bone and was easy to remove. If he rests, I'm happy it will heal without further intervention from a physician.'

Hester smiled wearily. 'I'm relieved to hear you say so. There's still a blizzard blowing at the moment and I doubt if anyone, however willing, will be able to get to town for a day or two.'

Hester heard the sound of footsteps approaching and hurried to open the door. 'Thank you, girls, I've cleared a space on the table for you.' She smiled at James now decently dressed, his arm in a sling but otherwise as cheerful as usual. 'I see there's tea as well as chocolate, James. Which would you prefer?'

'Tea would be grand, miss, and some of that plum cake to go with it, thank you.'

'Miss Frobisher, you sit down and let me and Meg serve; it's not right for you to wait on us.'

'If you insist, Polly, then I shall do so. I should like some of everything and chocolate to drink, please.'

The trays and the chocolate jug were almost empty when they heard footsteps on the stairs. Jet raised his head and thumped his tail and Hester relaxed, waiting to see who would emerge through the door praying it would be Ralph, and disappointed when Tom appeared.

'Miss Frobisher, his lordship says to tell you everything is under control. All the men who have been attacking us over the past few days have been dealt with. Seth, Robert and I will help ourselves to the supper you've left out. No doubt you're going to retire soon?'

She understood that this was more a suggestion than a question. Why should he want them … then she recalled the fact that there were several corpses to dispose of, not something he would wish to do in front of them. 'I've finished and am off to my bedchamber. Perhaps you could assist James to his before you go back downstairs, Tom.'

She stood up knowing the other three would be obliged to follow. Leaving Birdie to arrange matters with the girls, she retreated to her room. She could hear the murmur of voices and the clatter of crockery as Birdie directed the maids.

Ralph walked over to check the bolts on the inside of the trap were firmly across; he wanted to be certain no one else could break in. It was possible the rest of the gang might come to investigate when their comrades failed to return, but he thought the blizzard raging outside would keep them away tonight. Tomorrow, whatever the weather, he would take the fight to them.

'It would be easier if we had a chair to tie this bastard to, sir. Shall I attach him to a wall beam instead?'

'Here, let me give you a hand.'

The man smelt rank. Ralph's nostrils curled in disgust as he assisted in hoisting the inert form upright and lashing it to a couple of beams. 'Do we have water to throw over him?'

'I collected some snow in their slop pail when I opened the trap, it's melted a bit and will wake him up better than water.'

Ralph stepped back allowing Robin to hurl the contents of the slop bucket over their semi-conscious captive. The man groaned and his eyes flickered open. His gaze was vacant as he stared around the chamber, until he spotted the body and then comprehension dawned. It was time to commence the interrogation.

Without a second's hesitation Ralph stepped up and punched the man hard enough to split his lip, but not enough to render him senseless. He saw the victim's head snap back and his eyes widen in fear. 'I am Colebrook. I wish to know the whereabouts and identity of the man who sent you here to murder me.'

For a moment he stepped in close and raised his fist to strike again. The man's bladder emptied, splashing noisily on to the beaten earth of the floor. Ralph moved sideways avoiding the noisome puddle and felt a flicker of sympathy for the humiliated man hanging limp and defenceless. He hardened his resolve. He was a soldier and this man would have cut his throat without compunction given the slightest chance.

'I'm waiting. Don't make me ask the question a second time.'

The man's head jerked upright and words tumbled from his lips. The gentleman behind the attempts was renting a house a couple of miles away, Bracken Manor. There were a further six men there to scare away whoever remained alive.

'Cut him down, Robin, but make certain his bonds are secure. He can wait down here until the militia arrive to collect him.'

Robin completed his task and picked up a lantern. 'Do you wish to leave him with a candle?'

'No. He's fortunate to be alive, that's comfort enough.' He headed back along the tunnel, his thoughts whirling. There were still too many unanswered questions. He didn't know who lived at Bracken Manor nor how he came to know so much about this place. It had to be someone Aunt Agatha knew, a distant relative, someone who might have visited Neddingfield in the past and learnt its secrets.

He scowled. If his aunt had known of the existence of the passage she would have told them about it. This was a conundrum that wasn't going to be solved tonight. He was exhausted, his brain foggy; in the morning, after a good night's rest, no doubt he would come up with an explanation.

The faint flicker of light ahead told him they were approaching the exit. 'Robin, we shall not leave for the manor until I have made sense of what I've learned tonight.'

'Very well, my lord. Shall we meet in the library after breakfast?'

'Yes; the animals must be seen to, the snow cleared from the paths before we leave. I wonder, do Seth and Robert ride?'

'Doubt it, sir. But if the choice is walking thigh deep in snow or hanging on to a saddle, I reckon they'll manage right enough.'

The house was quiet, everyone asleep. There was a light coming from under the kitchen door and Ralph paused, had Hester ignored his instructions and waited up for him after all? His fatigue vanished and he threw open the door to discover it empty.

'Look, Robin, tea, brandy and food. Will you join me for supper?' He smiled, guessed who had arranged this welcome for him. The kettle was bubbling and whilst Robin made tea he pulled out a chair. After several slices of bread and ham, three cups of tea and a generous measure of brandy, he was feeling less fraught and more confident that morning would provide him with answers. Whoever it was, the man was a formidable opponent and he would need all his tactical skills to beat him.

At last! The sound of Jet banging his tail against her door told her Ralph must have returned safely. It couldn't be Tom, who was already in bed. She heard him pause, obviously fussing the dog, then his footsteps faded away and she heard the click of his bedchamber door.

The gentle snores coming from the bed of the far side of the room told her Birdie was sound asleep. Once her companion was in the land of nod she would remain there, unless shaken awake, for at least five hours. After that her friend would wake at the slightest noise; a life spent rising with the lark making her more responsive as dawn approached.

Hester wasn't sure how long to wait. She closed her eyes to visualize him taking off his outer garments, his boots, next his shirt ... and felt a flood of heat as a vivid picture of him first semi-clothed, then sitting naked on the end of his bed, made her tremble with an odd mix of fear and excitement.

Should she go now, or wait a while longer? A long delay

might mean her courage would fail her and Ralph might well be asleep. She swung her feet to the floor, not bothering to find her slippers, but just in case she met anyone slipped her arms into her robe. Her hair hung in a thick plait down almost to her waist – should she stop and loosen it? Like a wraith, she stole from her bedchamber closing the door quietly behind her.

'Hush now, Jet, I'm going to see Ralph. You must be a good boy and remain here silent.'

The animal heaved himself to his feet and padded along beside her. She hadn't bothered to bring a candle as she'd made sure the fire had been banked up before she'd gone to bed. The glow from the coals was more than enough to light her way.

She hesitated outside his door. Should she knock? What if he thought her an intruder and she was hurled to the ground as before? If she did, she might disturb the girls; sound travelled further in the silence of the night. No, she would have to slip in and close the door behind her before she announced her presence and pray she remained unharmed.

Chapter Eighteen

RALPH TOSSED HIS boots away, peeled down his britches flinging them on to the floor also; too damned tired to bother about niceties. He yawned, stretching his aching arms above his head. He was getting too old for this and sincerely hoped this was the last time his military skills would be called upon. His taste for violence, killing, had gone; what had occurred had left behind a sour taste.

Relaxing on the bed, certain tonight he would be instantly asleep, his eyes began to close. As he settled back, he tensed without sitting up, his eyes opened and focused on the door. Yes! There it was, a faint sound, the door was opening. My God! What now? How could the bastards have got in after all his closing of trapdoors and barricading of windows? He didn't have his pistol with him, no weapon of any sort and would have to rely on his bare hands.

Alert, his head clear, he waited to pounce on this unwary attacker who would be expecting him to be oblivious. Breathing in slowly through his nose, making no sound, he sighed: he knew that aroma as well as his own. A different kind of excitement flooded through him.

'Come in, my darling, an unexpected visit, but nonetheless a welcome one.'

*

His words coming from the darkness made Hester jump, and the door slammed shut. The noise echoed, and she paused, waiting to hear Birdie's voice calling out, or Tom clattering downstairs to investigate. He was holding his breath as well. There was a faint creak and he was beside her.

All her wild imaginings had not prepared her for the true splendour of his nakedness. The logs were burning bright and threw a red glow across his broad shoulders. She held her breath, she'd never seen anything so beautiful, so enticing. As if in a dream she raised one hand and her fingertips began to trace the outline of his muscles.

His skin was burning. The heat travelled up her outstretched fingers, along her arm and down to the very core of her being. Why didn't he move? Why didn't he say something? Had she offended him by coming to his chamber so brazenly? She should drop her hand, turn and flee before it was too late, but something held her there, unable to step back away from danger.

Ralph seemed to be having difficulty speaking – was he ill? His chest certainly was far hotter than it should be. 'Are you unwell, my love? Have you caught a chill from roaming around underground? You're trembling and I can feel your skin hot beneath my fingertips.'

Still he didn't move. Then finally he spoke, his voice deep and strained as though in pain. 'Sweetheart, I don't know what possessed you to come here like this, but unless you go this instant I shall be unable to hold back. I burn for *you*, darling. I want to make love to you, make you mine, smother you with kisses, bury myself deep inside you and hear you cry out my name.'

She wasn't quite sure of the exact meaning of his whispered words, but his sincerity and passion was clear. Taking a steadying breath she explained why she had come.

'I decided earlier tonight, that if you came back I should come to you. Who knows what tomorrow brings? I want you to know how much I love you. If anything should happen to you then I shall have tonight to treasure.'

'You have not thought this through, my love. What we are about to do could result in a child. Have you considered how you will be viewed if you produce a bastard?'

A baby? She hadn't thought of that, but she vividly recalled the despair in a letter she had received just before setting out for Neddingfield. It had been from a married friend enduring her fourth confinement in as many years; it told her it only took a single visit from her husband to the marital bed to result in pregnancy.

Her lips curved at the possibility of holding his baby in her arms in nine months' time. 'I don't care. I love you, and if tonight means I have a child then so be it. I don't care one jot for society, and have more than enough to provide for myself and a baby.' She felt a bubble of laughter welling up. 'I must say, my love, that I would prefer it to be a legitimate offspring and that you were there to share in its upbringing.'

With something more like a groan than anything else he drew her tighter, until he was pressing every inch of her against his burning flesh. She could feel his arousal against her stomach and for a moment felt fear as well as passion. Then she forgot everything as he scooped her up and carried her across to his bed.

'Darling, I have dreamt every night since we met of being able to run my fingers through your hair. Allow me to release it for you.'

Deftly, he pulled off the ribbon allowing her hair to cascade around her shoulders. She loved the way his fingers dipped into it, letting her tresses flow. She swayed towards him, wanting to feel his heat again. Laughing he held her still.

'Wait a minute, my sweet, there's more to do before we make love. Both of us have items of clothing to remove.'

His hands took the edges of her wrap and slid it slowly over her shoulders sending shivers of anticipation down her spine. As it pooled around her feet his hands traced patterns on her back, moulding the shape of her buttocks, her waist, shoulders and then around her collarbone to grasp the ends of the ribbon that held her nightgown firm.

She froze; she hadn't realized she was to be naked, wasn't sure she was ready for such a revelation. He felt her hesitation and his fingers stilled.

'My darling, I want to feel your skin against mine, want to kiss every inch of you. When two people are in love, there can be nothing between them, not even the cotton of a nightgown.' He didn't wait for her response, his fingers took each end of the ribbon and released the bow by tugging it sharply.

It joined her robe on the floor and she was standing, naked as the day she was born, in front of a man she scarcely knew. She closed her eyes not wishing to see him remove his final garment. She was glad the room was not lit, only the flickering of the fire bathing them in a rosy glow.

There was no turning back, her reputation was gone. She was utterly ruined; whatever happened, if Ralph didn't make an honest woman of her, no one else would. She was a well-brought-up young lady – what had possessed her to behave like this?

It was too late to repine. She had made her decision and must live with the consequences. She was about to spend the night in the arms of the man she loved, loved so much she was willing to give him her most precious gift. This thought gave her courage and instead of flinching away in embarrassment she raised her head and stared back at him thoughtfully.

She stretched languorously, feeling sated, feeling like a woman. The fire had burned down and was now a mere flicker in the grate. Her head was resting against his shoulder, her legs tangled with his, his arm heavy across her breast. She had never been so happy. She wanted to lie there for ever, secure in his love,

A faint scratching noise at the door attracted her attention. What was it? The noise came again, a little louder. It was Jet; it was the noise he made when he wished to attract her attention.

'I have to go, my love, it must be almost dawn. Birdie will be waking up. She mustn't find me gone.'

She tried to wriggle out from under his arm but it tightened, holding her captive. She felt the rumble of laughter in his chest. 'An impossibility, my love. Miss Bird can hardly find you if you're gone.'

'Don't be awkward. You know exactly what I mean. I would prefer my whereabouts not to become common knowledge. I'm very fond of my companion and have no wish to embarrass her if it can be avoided.'

The weight of his arm lifted. 'In that case, darling, return at once to your room.'

'I would, but I'm stuck fast. I'm pinned beneath the covers on one side and by your bulk on the other. Kindly get out, my lord, so that I can also do so.'

'It is you who wish to remove yourself from this warm nest, my angel, not I. However, as a gentleman I'm obliged to accommodate your slightest wish.'

Two hands gripped her firmly about her middle and next thing she was sitting on her bottom, on the floor, whilst he remained snugly in bed.

Definitely not amused by his antics she scrabbled about until she located her nightgown and wrapper. Remaining on her knees, out of his view, she quickly donned her nightclothes. Her fingers were clumsy and refused to tie the bow so she dropped the ribbon and left it floating. Her hair was in the way, impatiently she tossed it behind her back.

'You cannot return with your hair like that, darling. Can you find the ribbon? I shall braid it for you whilst you search.'

She felt him smooth it back from her forehead and then, with nimble fingers, he began to plait. Silently she handed up the ribbon and felt a slight tug as he fastened it around the end. Although he had completed his task, she was strangely reluctant to move. Her limbs were heavy and she glowed all over from his touch.

After one night in his arms already she loved the feel of his hands on her body, loved the exquisite feeling he had given her as he'd kissed every inch of her. This would not do. If she sat here much longer he would fling off her nightgown and they would tumble back into bed to repeat the blissful experience of the night. There had been a little pain at first, but the pleasure that followed had more than made up for it.

'I shall be getting up very soon, darling. After the men have taken care of the livestock I shall lead my band of intrepid heroes across to Bracken Manor to confront the man behind all this. You're safe here. On my return I shall locate the vicar and arrange for our banns to be called which means we can be wed in three weeks.'

He sounded confident, didn't consider matters might go awry. He and Robin were the only ones trained to fight. Tom was a fine shot and could hold his own at fisticuffs, but he wasn't a soldier and neither were the two grooms. They were going to face six or more ex-soldiers who would be fighting for their lives.

A shudder of apprehension shook her and, sensing her distress, his arms came down to lift her from the rug, placing her on the edge of the bed whilst he cradled her.

'Please don't worry, my sweet. I know what I'm doing and we have surprise on our side. This matter has to be settled; I want to be able to spend my time with you, plan our lives together in peace, and we can't do that until this is settled.'

'I know, but for all your confidence, you're outnumbered and your men lack experience. I shall say no more on the subject. I shall remain here and busy myself with domestic duties and pray that you all return safely.'

'When it's over, I shall send Tom to fetch the militia. I promise you, everything will be over today.'

'What about the snow?'

'Listen, what can you hear?'

She cocked her head to one side. First all she could hear was the faint crackle of the fire and his steady breathing, then she heard something else: the sound of water against the window panes.

'Good heavens! There's been a thaw. If it's raining hard enough to hear then it must be heavy indeed.' She scrambled to her feet. Jet had accompanied his scratching with a faint bark, and she knew from bitter experience if she ignored him, he would start to howl and then all would be disaster. 'Take care, my love, and come back safe to me.'

She had said all she wished to say; he knew how she felt, that her very existence was in his hands, but there was a job to do and she would not expedite matters by remaining weeping at his side.

The sitting area was deserted, only her huge dog there to witness her disgrace. She walked over to the fire and threw some logs on the burning embers; she had no wish to go back to bed, to pretend to be asleep. When Birdie emerged at dawn it would be to find her curled up on the *chaise-longue*, her pet beside her, reading a novel.

Jet having completed his greeting seemed content to flop down across her toes. She was relieved he didn't wish to be let out, as she didn't have the energy to struggle with the heavy bolts on the door just then.

She sat for ten minutes before becoming chilled. She would

have to go back to bed; it was nonsensical to remain out here. In any case she ought not to be sitting here when the men got up.

'You stay here, boy, I'm going back to bed. Ralph can let you out when he rises.'

She crept back inside her chamber, carefully arranging her robe on the end of her bed before climbing in. Her feet were frozen and she tucked them inside her nightgown, under the thickness of her comforter slowly thawing out, but she couldn't relax. Her eyes brimmed as she contemplated a life without him at her side; her dreams were not filled with images of delight but of death and despair.

She didn't hear him leave his room and head downstairs to discuss his plans for the attack on Bracken Manor, not stirring until Miss Bird shook her gently by the shoulder.

'Wake up, my dear. You'll be delighted to hear that the snow's gone. We shall be free to leave this place today.'

Chapter Nineteen

'LEAVE? I HAVE no wish to leave, Birdie. Lord Colebrook and I are to be married as soon as the banns are read – we cannot possibly leave Neddingfield until after our nuptials.'

'Congratulations, my dear. Although I believe it's more customary to congratulate the gentleman when a couple become betrothed. Do you think you have given yourself enough time to be sure your affections are engaged? After all, you've known each other for less than a sennight.'

'I have never been more certain of anything in my life. We're a perfect match. We haven't known each other long, but have experienced more in the past few days than most couples do in a lifetime.'

She turned her back on her mentor under the pretext of slipping into her chemise, as she had no wish for her secret to be revealed. She hadn't had time to examine her face in the glass, but was certain there would be tell-tale signs that she was no longer an innocent.

'I heard his lordship go down. I should think all the fires are lit and the range burning by now.'

The sound of footsteps passing the door made her hurry her morning ablutions. Polly and Meg could not be expected to do everything themselves; the fact that she was about to become a countess made no never mind. She would do her part until they were able to re-staff the hall.

'Go down, Birdie, I shall be there directly. With luck the men have found themselves breakfast and we'll only have ourselves to prepare for.'

It was strange, her appearance no longer mattered; Ralph loved her and even in her oldest garments she knew she would be beautiful to him. Her mood swung from elation at the thought of what had passed between them to despair as she worried about what might happen when he confronted their nemesis.

He had told her the bad men had been discussing quite callously how they had been paid to murder them both. It was strange that they had killed no one so far; the only killing had been done by them. Was it possible he had misheard? What sort of person could it be who was prepared to pay to have two people murdered in cold blood but then hold back when it came to their employees?

She felt her stomach roil as she remembered pulling the trigger on the pistol and watching the man stagger away to die. Had the men merely been going to abduct them? She shivered and pulled her shawl tighter. No; what possible use would they be as prisoners? There would have been no one left to pay their ransom for Aunt Agatha had already left the country. However hard it was to understand that a stranger should wish her dead, she was forced to accept this was the only possible explanation.

The man was a ruthless murderer. His only motive was to remove them from his path and give him access to the title and their fortunes. What if ... She shook her head. This would not do. She would run mad thinking of what might happen. Her hair successfully arranged on top of her head, she was ready to go down. Keeping herself busy baking and attending to James should help her forget about the danger Ralph was in.

The kitchen was redolent with the smell of baking bread and frying ham. The kettle was boiling, the plates and cutlery laid out for breakfast, but the room was empty. For a moment she felt a lurch of fear then smiled at her nonsense. The girls would be in the dairy milking the cows and Birdie would be … where would she be? She heard the door to the root cellar bang shut and relaxed. 'Do you require any help with the vegetables?'

Her friend appeared, a smudge of dirt on her nose, a basket bulging with potatoes, onions and carrots. 'Thank you, my dear, I have everything I need for soup. Would you like to wait until the bread is ready? The ham and eggs are done to a turn and you could make toast to eat with it.'

Hester removed the long-handled, three pronged fork from the hook by the range and pulling up a chair speared a piece of yesterday's bread on the end. 'Shall I toast all this? Have you and the girls eaten this morning?'

'We haven't, but do enough only for yourself. It wouldn't be seemly for the girls to eat with you and I'm far too busy at the moment.'

After eating her solitary breakfast Hester offered to carry a tray up to James. His more personal needs had been dealt with by Tom so she wouldn't be expected to do anything other than keep him company.

The young man seemed inordinately pleased to see her. 'Miss Bird insists that I stay put today. I'm going daft with boredom, Miss Frobisher. There's much I have to tell you and we haven't had the opportunity to talk yet.'

'You must eat your meal first. I'm quite content to sit and stare into the fire until you finish.' She wondered what news he had; she had no wish to know the sordid details of his incarceration and couldn't imagine what else there might be he had to tell her.

The clatter of his tray being dropped on to the floor startled her from her reverie. 'You should have asked me to help you;

you're not supposed to put any stress on your shoulder.' She removed the remains of his breakfast to place it on the top of his chest of drawers. 'James, I shall bring my chair a little nearer so you can see me.'

'I know where Miss Culley is, and the rest of them,' he announced baldly. He had her undivided attention now.

'Tell me, James. I have been desperate for definite news.'

'I was that scared at first, thinking I was trapped by ghosts, but I overheard them talking together. I reckon they forgot I was listening and their voices carried down that tunnel. I knew then they were mortals, just like me.' He paused, making the most of his moment. 'Lord Colebrook was right: they did dress up as soldiers. They marched to Neddingfield and told Miss Culley that her sympathies towards the French had been noted in Whitehall and she was going to be arrested as a traitor. She was given the choice of going into permanent exile and she took it. The devils laughed about it; they enjoyed the fact they'd tricked her into leaving.'

Hester could hardly credit that someone as awake to every suit should be gulled in this way. There was only one reason that would have prompted her intrepid aunt to leave in such a precipitous fashion. What she and Ralph had feared, had to be true – or at least partially so.

'It seems incredible that her staff agreed to accompany her. At least one of them, Sam Roberts, was supposedly a follower of Polly's. The poor girl will be devastated he abandoned her so easily.'

'I shouldn't worry too much about her, miss; from what Tom said I think there's already something between the two of them. She'll not be lonely for long if he has his way.'

'I hope his intentions are honourable.' She watched him turn an unbecoming shade of beetroot.

'He wants to marry the girl, miss, you have my word on that.'

'I am relieved to hear you say so.' She wandered across to look out of the window at the dripping landscape. She could hardly believe the snow had melted overnight leaving only piles of slush where it had been deepest. It was a depressing sight, the sky overcast, the trees drooping and dismal.

'My word! There's a closed carriage just turned into the gate. If I'm to receive visitors I'd better go downstairs and make myself respectable. Do you have everything you need, James?'

'Yes, thank you, Miss Frobisher. Tom left me some pieces of wood and I have my penknife – I thought I might carve a few animals to pass the time, but I can't do it one-handed. I shall rest and watch the flames until someone has time to keep me company.'

Hester checked her hair was neat, her skirts free of cobwebs and dust and went to wait in the makeshift drawing-room. Being careful not to dirty her hands she threw several more logs on to the fire and gave it a rattle with the poker. The cheery blaze made the space seem more acceptable.

She hadn't been waiting long before Polly burst in, a trifle breathless after her dash up the stairs. 'Miss Frobisher, there's visitors from London come to see you and Lord Colebrook. Miss Bird wants to know if she should send them away, or if you'll see them on your own.' The girl grinned. 'At the moment they're standing under the back porch trying to shelter from the rain and the door's firmly shut. Miss Bird won't budge until you've given permission.'

The carriage had come from the direction of Little Neddingfield, and if the gentlemen had asked to speak to both her and Lord Colebrook she was sure it was something to do with Aunt Agatha. 'Please have them come up here. Ask Meg to bring refreshments; I shall require you to remain with me, Polly.'

The girl dipped. 'It's a good thing Miss Bird has baked this morning or there would be nothing suitable to offer them.'

Fifteen minutes later the sound of heavy footsteps and the murmur of well-modulated voices was evident in the stairwell. It was only then Hester began to fear she might have made a dreadful mistake and invited the enemy into the very heart of the Hall.

It was still dark when Ralph addressed his inadequate band of heroes. They were gathered in the wavering lamplight in the warmth of the stable block. Robin and Tom he could rely on, as they had already proved their mettle, but his driver, Fred, was too old for this kind of action and Seth and Robert had no experience of firearms.

'You already know where we're going and why, are there any further questions you wish to ask before we leave?'

The men looked at Robin who had resumed as second-in-command now that the matter of ghosts had been laid to rest. 'It's like this, my lord, how do we know what that man said about the number at Bracken Manor is right? I'm not saying he was lying, but he's not been there, and more men could have joined the gang.'

'It's possible, but unlikely. Until this morning the roads were impassable and if reinforcements have been sent for they can't be there before us. I remember the Manor from a previous visit; it's more isolated than here. Remember, we've the edge; they're not expecting us.'

He nodded a dismissal and turned to tighten Thunder's girths, leaving Robin to organize the others. He swung into the saddle unhindered by his sword; his years of practice during the war made it look easier than it was. Today Robin was also armed with a cavalry sword as well as his pistols. They both knew how to use them.

The stable doors were open and he urged his mount through, and the others clattered behind. Seth and Robert were competent horsemen and had cudgels strapped to their saddles; they had shown him the wicked knives secreted in their top boots. Ralph knew he would be in a better position if he had a couple of riflemen along, but it was too late now to worry. He would succeed with what he had; he had no choice.

The wild ride across country was unpleasant. His tricorn hat and heavy riding coat were scarcely adequate to keep out the driving rain. He had issued weatherproof coats to the three men and was glad that he'd had the forethought to do so. He needed all his men alert and responsive not frozen to the marrow.

The first grey light of dawn greeted their arrival on the narrow track that bordered the grounds of Bracken Manor. He wasn't sure how well secured the premises were, or if his opponent would have the sense to post sentries. He would have done so, but then he was a cautious man. He raised his arm. He swung his horse round to face them and they gathered near in order to hear, the lashing rain meant his words barely carried.

'If my memory serves me, there's a small path running into the park and it's this we're taking. The horses must stay here and shelter under these trees; it's barely adequate but it will have to serve. Remember we mustn't be seen. Pull your hats down and cover your faces with your mufflers. Whatever you do, don't look up, if anyone is watching that will give us away.'

Fred was taking care of the horses; he would remain there and carry a message to the local magistrate, Squire Norton, if they failed to return within the hour. It was not foolproof, but the best he could do.

Bertram Sinclair knew that by the end of the day he would be the rightful Earl of Waverly. the obstacles that presently stood in his way would have been removed and he would be able to take himself to London, resume the life of wealthy man about town and wait to hear with suitable surprise that the title was his.

His men had their instructions. It had taken them until the night before last to master the intricate mechanism that opened the way into Neddingfield Hall. Until that was done he'd had to bide his time, do all he could to terrify the remaining occupants, but had been unable to complete his masterly scheme.

This and the snow had been as much a hindrance to him as it had been to the major. His men needed to dispose of the witnesses, all five of them if necessary, and then they could release the man held captive. They would transport him to where he had been taken and leave him to run babbling, back to the Hall but he would discover it deserted. This time he'd sent two of his own men down to the cellar; this was not a job to leave to hirelings, they'd tell him what he wanted to hear just to get his money.

A strong gust of wind sent smoke billowing out from the chimney and he retreated, as he had done countless times before, coughing and swearing. Whilst waiting for the room to clear he walked over to the window, the draught whistling through easing his lungs. There were no curtains and the shutters were in sore need of repair, which is why he kept candles to a minimum, he wanted no one to know that Bracken Manor was occupied.

The smoke from the kitchen range and his own fire might well have been seen, but hopefully those who saw it would assume vagrants had taken occupation for the winter and would not investigate too closely. As long as no busybody called out the militia he was safe.

Jones had instructions to kill the girl and her companion as well as the major, and if necessary anyone else whom they thought might blab. The bodies were to be taken back through the secret tunnel and buried in the cellar, the brandy barrels stacked on top of the makeshift grave.

It was thirty years since the smugglers had used this hidey-hole and he doubted that even they would dare to come close to a place where people mysteriously disappeared in the night and ghostly howling and flashing lights were seen. His lips twisted in a smile. That dog the men had spoken of was adding to the atmosphere of menace.

Hester wished she'd kept her pistol, but she'd returned it to Ralph the previous day believing she had had no further use for it. Where was Jet? He was as good as any pistol – hadn't he already killed two men?

Her heart thumped and she clenched her fingers in her lap. She would send Polly to look for the dog, convention might dictate she shouldn't be alone with one gentleman, let alone two, but everything was topsy-turvy at the moment. She rose gracefully as the door opened, pausing as Polly announced the visitors as though she was ushering them into the drawing-room and not an overlarge hallway in the servants' quarters.

'Mr Siddon and Mr Siddon are here to see you, Miss Frobisher.'

Both men were elderly, and if there was anything villainous about either of them she would eat her best straw bonnet. She stepped forward nodding her head in greeting. 'Gentlemen, it's a pleasure to see you. I must apologize for the unusual accommodation, but we are sadly understaffed so had no alternative but to close down the Hall.'

Mr Siddon, the senior of the two brothers, bowed formally. 'Thank you for agreeing to see us, Miss Frobisher. We're Miss Culley's lawyers; it's on her instructions we're here. We were aware that you have no staff and have come to explain why she was obliged to leave you in such a predicament.'

'Pray be seated, gentlemen.' She sat and waited for them to arrange themselves side-by-side on the day-bed. They looked like a pair of black crows sitting on a fence. 'I have been told that my aunt has removed to the Continent and has taken her staff with her.'

The two exchanged glances and nodded sagely. 'Exactly that, Miss Frobisher. Your aunt has long been a dear friend of ours and we're sorry to see her go. However, there are other things I need to explain to you.' The two exchanged looks a second time. 'We understand that fortuitously his lordship is also staying at Neddingfield Hall. We had hoped to be able to speak to Lord Colebrook also, but he's not here.'

She hid a smile behind her hand. Did they think she hadn't noticed his absence? 'We're to be married in three weeks' time, so it's in order for you to give me any information you might have.'

'In that case, Miss Frobisher, we see no obstacle.' More nods and looks. They were becoming more farcical by the minute. 'Your aunt has settled the property jointly on you both – I have the title deeds here to give you. You're to do as you wish with the estate. Miss Culley has no objection to you selling it, though she would prefer you to make your home here.'

'It's certainly a possibility. We shall be here for the next few weeks as we intend to marry at the church.'

The rattle of cups heralded the arrival of the promised refreshments. Polly rushed across in a flurry of skirts and held the door open for Meg to stagger in with a laden tray. Over tea and hot scones she discovered that the lawyers had been snowed in and had been happily ensconced at the Jug and Bottle.

'Gentlemen, do you intend to return directly from here to Town, or shall you be staying a further night at the inn?'

'We shall stay one more night there, Miss Frobisher; it's most comfortable and the food plentiful and excellent. Indeed, it has been almost like a little holiday for us.'

'In that case, sir, would you do me a favour? I should like you to take three letters with you. Mr Jarvis can send one of the potboys with them. I've not written them yet, so could I ask you to remain for a little while longer whilst I do so?'

The elder Mr Siddon replied. So far all his younger brother had done was nod and smile. 'We shall be delighted to wait. Could we possibly have a little more tea and some more of these delicious scones whilst we sit by this delightful fire?'

'Of course; Polly shall go downstairs immediately and fetch fresh. The missives are short; it will not take me many minutes to accomplish my task.'

In the privacy of her shared bedchamber she opened her escritoire. Relieved she had a pen with a decent point she removed the cork from the ink bottle and wrote her first note. This was to the vicar, one Mr Blunt. In it she requested that he attend Neddingfield Hall in order to arrange for the banns to be called.

The second was to the local magistrate, Squire Norton, briefly explaining what had been happening over the past days and asking him to call out the militia and arrange for the removal of the corpses from the outhouse.

The third was to Mrs Jarvis asking if she could spread the word that there had been no ghosts at the Hall, but villains, and to ask the staff who had abandoned them if they would like to return. She sanded the paper and folded each, carefully sealing them with a small blob of wax melted with a candle flame.

The lawyers departed replete with scones and conserve and with the promise to see the notes were delivered to Mr Jarvis. Satisfied she had done all she could to help she went downstairs to talk to Birdie about the visit.

'It's almost ten o'clock, why hasn't Lord Colebrook returned? He promised me this visit to Bracken Manor wouldn't take long.' She stopped, horrified by her mistake, praying the revelation that she'd seen Ralph last night might pass unnoticed. It did not.

She saw her companion's expression change. She waited for

the bear garden jaw to start, but instead the air was rent by a hideous scream and Meg fell into the kitchen her face covered with blood.

Chapter Twenty

THANK GOD THE rain had stopped. Ralph knew it would be far easier to negotiate the quagmire that faced them without the added misery of horizontal rain. He viewed the stretch of open ground with disfavour. It was the only section in which they would be visible if they walked upright. However, by slithering across on their bellies they would be screened by the laurel hedge that bordered the kitchen garden.

He checked his pistols were secure, then twisted his sword belt so the blade rested in the small of his back. His heavy riding coat was so long it reached almost to his feet, and with luck it would keep the worst of the mud from his person.

Dropping to his knees, he began the slow, messy business of transferring himself, like an overlarge slug, across the mud bath. The sound of muttered curses came from behind, but he knew no one balked at their unusual method of progress.

By using his forearms and toes his body was kept mostly clear of the ground, and he hoped the others were as successful. The brown sludge began to seep through the thick material of his cloak and his pace increased. Arriving breathless, although relatively dry, in the shelter of the bushes he rose to a crouch then ran to the rear of the kitchen garden to wait for the others to catch up.

The front of his riding cape was heavy with mud so it was discarded. He would have had to remove it in order to fight anyway, so it made little difference leaving it here. His topcoat would have to suffice for the rest of this excursion. His lips twitched as he swivelled his sword back into place on his left hip and checked his pistols were dry.

When his men were assembled behind him, their filthy coats heaped beside his own, he went over their next move. This was a critical part of the exercise. They had to reach the house undetected; they were outnumbered and could be picked off by rifle fire if spotted.

Making sure everyone was ready, they began the slow creep forward along the far end of the hedge, down an overgrown path towards the outbuildings. He assumed Robin and Tom were close behind him and the grooms were bringing up the rear. The noise of stamping and chomping coming from the stone building, the clanking of buckets and occasional muffled shout told him it was the stables.

Were these innocent servants, or part of the murderous gang? It made no difference; they had to be overcome, gagged and restrained. Apologies, if needed, would be given later. He beckoned for Robin and Tom to follow and for the other two to wait and, keeping his head down, his muffler fixed around his face, he hoped his dark topcoat would make him blend into the grey walls.

He paused to peer through an unglazed window. As expected, there were two men taking water to the beasts inside – most of the stalls were occupied but he thought there were no more than a dozen horses, not the expected eighteen or so.

Did the half-empty stables indicate that men had already left to investigate why their comrades had not returned triumphant the night before? It was too late to turn back; he was committed. His attack would be swift, and *if* things had gone awry, they could gallop back and be in time to prevent a tragedy.

He ran round to the stable doors, pulling out his pistol,

holding it by the barrel, intending to use the handle as a club. The two grooms were knocked unconscious without a murmur; they didn't see him coming.

'Tie them up, stuff rags in their mouths, I don't want them shouting a warning. Find an empty storeroom and dump them.' He turned to Robin, speaking quietly to him. 'I think I might have made a grievous error; it's possible that as we rode here some men left and are on their way to Neddingfield. We must do this quickly; Hester's life depends on our return.'

He knew if the bastards got hold of her he would capitulate and they would have lost. He would willingly give his own life, and anyone else's, in order to keep her safe.

The rear of the building was the best place through which to secure a safe entry, as the staff working there would be less likely to be armed. His boots were so clogged with mud that his feet stuck unpleasantly every step he took and he paused to scrape them clean. The kitchen door was unlocked and he pushed it open, listening, poised to move in an instant. All he heard was silence.

He slipped around the doorjamb into a deserted passageway. God, it was cold in here! There was the clatter of pots and pans in a room off to his left. He indicated that Seth and Robert should deal with whoever was in there. With a pistol in each hand, ready to fire, he ran light-footed into the main part of the house. His breath steamed in front of him and he wondered what sort of man was prepared to live so frugally and yet employ a dozen or so men to commit murder at his behest.

Keeping to the edge of the flagged hall, he inched his way towards the sound of voices coming from the closed doors ahead of him. This must be the main drawing-room; if it was, there should be doors to the rear that led to the dining-room. He gestured to Robin and Tom and mouthed the words *dining-room*. Robin nodded and ran off down the next passageway to locate a second entrance.

Ralph was ready, his pulse normal, hands dry, eyes like green glass. This was the moment he'd been waiting for these past two weeks, the denouement, and he prayed it would not be just a confrontation, but an end.

He stepped close to the doors, pressing his ear against the crack and listened. Yes, there were at least two people inside. He closed his eyes trying to imagine the precise whereabouts of the men in the room. They were not by the windows, so they must be in front of the fireplace.

Transferring both guns temporarily to his left hand he released the catch that held the doors, then returned the pistol. Taking a deep breath, he raised his boot and smashed the door open, bursting into the room his pistols pointed in the direction of the voices.

The two men nearest to him were dressed in plain cloth coats, britches and poorly cleaned top boots – these were hirelings, not the master. As they spun round, mouths agape, he fired. His aim was deadly and they both tumbled to the floor to join their comrades in Hades. Pushing his useless firearms into his belt he drew his sword in a single sweep and before the man who had caused him so much grief could do more than blink he was facing death at the end of the blade.

'On your knees.'

The man collapsed in an abject heap at his feet, visibly shaking, defeated. Ralph felt a rush of relief – it was over. He had forgotten his earlier qualms, forgotten that there were other men riding towards Neddingfield at this very moment.

This quivering object at his feet was the man behind it all; he glared at him with interest. Could this nondescript person be the monster he was seeking? He heard a noise behind him and glanced sharply over his shoulder; it was Tom and Robin coming in through the double doors that led from the dining-room.

'Find some rope and tie him up, then get something stuffed in his mouth.' He turned back and prodded the heap on the carpet with his sword. 'Get up, you snivelling coward – sit on that chair. I have questions for you and you will answer if you wish to live.'

His erstwhile opponent scrabbled, crablike, to the chair and hoisted himself on to it like a penitent child. The man kept his head lowered, his thin shoulders shaking visibly.

'Who are you? What's your name?'

The man's head jerked up and Ralph recoiled. Before his eyes his captive transformed into a slim man, a little older than himself, no more a gibbering wreck than he was. The hate that blazed back at him reminded him forcibly of the missing men.

'My name is Lord Colebrook, or it will be before this day is done.' The voice was clipped, aristocratic in tone; everything was explained by those few words. Ralph's throat filled with bile and he swallowed. The laugh that followed was the sound of a madman. 'Gag him. Throw him in the nearest closet. We have to get back; we have no time to waste here.'

They roughly trussed the man and carried him out to the hall. There was more likelihood of a cupboard at the rear of the manor, and Ralph went ahead, frantically opening doors until he found a boot room and they tossed him in. The putative earl was safely incarcerated. He looked up as Seth and Robert appeared from the kitchen.

'Is everything secure in there?'

'Yes, my lord. There was a simpleton and an old fellow; we locked them in the cellar; they'll raise no alarms down there.'

'Good. We have to get back, the other men are on their way to Neddingfield. There's no time to return for our mounts, we shall have to take horses from the stables.'

He crashed out of the back door and ran to the stables, saddling his own mount. Not waiting to see if the others were ready, he vaulted aboard and kicked the horse into a gallop. He hadn't paused to reload his pistols but his sword was safely back in its scabbard.

The mud sprayed up from the puddles and the icy wind removed his hat. He didn't notice the cold. With every hoofbeat he willed the animal faster, knowing that however hard he rode he could be too late.

Birdie screamed and stepped forward to help the girl. Hester, guessing what was to follow, turned and fled from the room. Something had gone horribly wrong with Ralph's plan, instead of finding and defeating the villains he'd missed them altogether. They were here. They had come to kill her. If she could hide until he returned maybe they wouldn't hurt the others.

Her present quarters would be the first place they'd look, so, instead, she ran into the hall and headed up the staircase that dominated the hall. Her skirts were bunched in front of her, her breath steaming as she hurried. She wasn't sure where to hide, just knew it had to be somewhere they wouldn't think to look. That ruled out her apartment and her aunt's. She would go to Ralph's; he slept at the rear of the house somewhere.

With luck they wouldn't look there, at least not immediately. A well-bred young lady wouldn't enter a gentleman's bedchamber under any circumstances. These men couldn't know that matters had changed, to them she would be a distant cousin, a young girl more used to sitting at her tatting than brutally killing one of their own.

At least she hoped that's what they'd think. She looked back to check there were no footprints on the carpet to mark her progress, before slipping into his large parlour. There was nothing here to hide behind. The window seat was too small, and although there were several octagonal tables, a writing desk, a tall clock, none of these would give her efficient protection from more than a cursory search.

What about his bedchamber? An enormous tester bed dominated the room, a flight of steps positioned at the end to allow access to the interior, the heavy brocade curtains, looped back, surrounding it. This might be the ideal place; a ruffle of matching material edged the bed frame and this would conceal a space large enough to crawl in to.

Dropping to her knees she peered under. It would be a tight squeeze, but if she wriggled to the very centre when anyone looked under the bed they wouldn't see her. She thanked God that she was dressed in a serviceable navy gown, its waist where it should be and the skirt allowing her freedom of movement.

Hester was preparing to slither under sideways when she noticed the thick layer of dust and realized at once that if anyone looked they would see from the disturbance someone was underneath. This was not the place; she rolled away, standing to shake out her dress. The far door led into the dressing-room where she found a series of huge closets, the first had a rail with several of Ralph's top coats; on the shelves were some folded shirts and undergarments.

Stepping in behind the clothes she pulled the door shut behind her. It was suffocatingly dark; but his familiar smell comforted her, calming her, making her ready to face whatever might happen in the next half-hour. She fingered her way along the rear of the closet, not pausing until she reached the shelves.

She was pressed hard against the wall and reached out a hand. To her surprise it floated in midair. Was this the perfect place? Whoever had constructed the shelves hadn't taken them to the back wall, there was a narrow space, about twelve inches deep, just big enough for her to squeeze in to.

She was glad she was slender, but she wished her breasts were not so generous, as they squashed uncomfortably against the back of the shelves. There was a risk of becoming stuck, but it was a more attractive alternative than being captured by the ruthless men downstairs. Hester edged deeper and deeper into the crevice until her shoulder abutted the end of the closet.

The dark was overpowering, she could only breathe in shallow gasps and understood, too late, that she might have made a dreadful error. If obliged to remain long she might be unable to extricate herself.

At least there was no worry that her legs would give way beneath her, being so tightly jammed in her hidey-hole she could raise her feet from the floor and still remain upright. She closed her eyes and tried to think of Ralph.

Chapter Twenty-one

RALPH HAULED ON the reins and his foam-flecked horse dropped back to a canter, then to a stumbling walk. He knew the beast was done; he'd driven it hard and it wasn't as fit as it should be. He could see the shape of the outbuildings ahead and behind them the massive bulk of Neddingfield.

He dropped on the ground; feet slipping from under him and grabbed at his stirrup leather to keep himself upright. 'Bloody hell! Leave the horses, we walk from here.'

For the second time that morning he crouched, pulling the collar of his topcoat up and readjusting the muffler so that it covered his face. He threaded his way through the dripping branches listening for any sound that would indicate they had been observed.

Waving Robin to take one side of the stable block, he took the other; Tom would follow with the grooms. He hadn't seen any evidence the Hall was occupied, but this didn't mean the villains weren't there. They were ex-soldiers and knew how to disguise their passage.

He reached the yard, scanning it cautiously; it was empty, still no sign of intruders. He paused to reload his pistols. Certain he was right, they were here somewhere, he couldn't relax for a second. If they were in the house they would have entered through the back door – would they have guarded it?

Keeping low, he ran across the yard and began his slow approach. Still no sign. He froze. What was that? He heard a low rumbling sound and recognized it instantly. It was Jet, and he wasn't happy. The dog was prowling around outside the house, his hackles up and growling continuously. This confirmed his worst suspicions. The men were inside. Looking over his shoulder he saw that Robin understood. His face bleak, he stopped, pressing himself into the shadows.

Robin arrived at his side. 'What now, my lord? They'll have the kitchen garden watched. But there's no voices, no screaming, maybe they've not found Miss Frobisher.'

'Yes, but that doesn't solve the problem of how we're going to effect an entry. We can't approach the rear and all the shutters and doors are locked on the ground floor. Let me think.' He shut his eyes trying to visualize the layout of the house. 'We can get in though my aunt's chambers, there's a creeper runs up the corner of the building. I can climb in that way.'

'You'll not do it alone, sir. If Tom and I follow you, Seth and Robert can guard the back and if anyone comes out the dog will help deal with them.'

Ralph nodded. He had to assume that there would be two men in the kitchen area, which meant four searching for Hester. If he could get in before they were discovered they would not be drastically outnumbered.

He waved his hand indicating they reverse and they regrouped behind the dairy block. He explained his plan, checking they understood their part in it. It would be easier to reach the front of the building via the rose garden; there was more cover and less likelihood of them being spotted from an upstairs window.

Arriving at the corner of the building he stared – it was no more than twenty feet or so. At this end of the house the windows had been changed from small leaded casements to large sash windows. He tested the rigidity of the plant before attempting to climb. It seemed firm enough. Reaching above his head to grasp a branch, he swung his feet from the ground. With surprising agility for a man of his size he shot upwards and was on to the wide window sill in seconds. The one thing he'd not considered was that the catch might be pulled across. Then he'd have to break the glass in order to enter which was bound to warn any men in the vicinity.

He breathed again – thank the good Lord – the window was unfastened. Balancing precariously, sliding his knife into the gap between the frame and the window ledge, he jerked the knife down, to use it as a lever. The window moved up an inch or two allowing him to get his fingers underneath. He replaced his knife and, gripping the window, slowly raised it.

It didn't screech or stick. He dropped his leg over into the space between the window and the shutters; the heavy brocade curtains were drawn and peering through them it was obvious the room was empty. Had it been searched already? He moved to one side as Robin arrived soundlessly, followed by Tom. There was a slight grating sound as it shut. If the window was left open there could be a draught which would move the curtains.

He waited a minute before easing the shutters apart and slipping between them. Then leant against the wall to remove his boots, not taking the risk of being heard on uncarpeted floors. A slight shuffling indicated the others were doing the same. He drew his sword and dropped it back into the scabbard, cocked both pistols, the sound loud in the empty room.

Tom and Robin placed their boots behind the shutters then he led them around the perimeter of his aunt's private parlour to the door that led into the corridor. His hands tightened on his weapons. There were footsteps approaching.

*

The walls of her prison seemed to be moving closer. Hester tried to ease the pressure from her chest, but was stuck fast. A wave of panic almost overwhelmed her; from somewhere she found the courage to force it away.

She knew if she struggled her breathing would be more restricted and she was like to suffocate. As long as she remained calm, took small shallow breaths, relaxed her limbs, all would be well. Someone, either the intruders or Ralph would find her. Birdie and Polly had seen her vanish, knew she was hiding, so all she had to do was remain calm and try to think about happier times.

Her toes and fingers were the only part of her anatomy she could move. She wriggled them vigorously. It wasn't cold, that was a blessing. A strange feeling of lethargy began to overcome her and her head pounded. Oh dear! This was a bad time to be developing a megrim. She forced herself to think about Ralph, about their future together, about their wedding day.

She would drift off to sleep for a while; her head was heavy, and she believed she was becoming quite accustomed to her confinement. Could she hear voices shouting? Never mind, whoever it was would come back when she'd had her nap.

Ralph saw the handle turning and raised his pistols. He was positioned directly in front, if the person opening it knew, he was as good as dead. However, if he didn't … his lips twisted in anticipation.

Robin was to his left, Tom to his right – they had both barrels of their weapons fixed firmly on the slowly moving door.

'We ain't looked in 'ere, 'ave we? Where the bleeding 'ell is she? Christ, it's as cold as a tomb up 'ere. With any luck she'll 'ave frozen to death and save us the trouble of topping 'er.'

The door opened wider, Ralph held his nerve, if he fired too soon it could prove fatal – to him – not to his opponents.

The person who had spoken continued to push into the room. The door swung fully open and Ralph saw two men, unshaven, both carrying guns, but neither having them cocked and ready to fire. His trigger finger tightened, but something stopped him; instead, he leapt forward, jamming his gun down the throat of the first man, hearing Robin and Tom do the same with the second.

'Not a sound if you want to live,' he snarled. The man remained mute. 'Drop your weapons.' Ralph swore under his breath; a bad move, if the others were within earshot they would be upon them in a moment. Without compunction he reversed his weapon and hit the man on the back of the head, catching him as he crumpled.

'Tie and gag them both, Tom. Quick, we might only have a minute or two before the others arrive.'

Robin dispatched the second intruder with cold-blooded efficiency. Leaving his minions to secure them, he pulled the door closed and put his eyes to the crack. His pulse steadied as he realized they were undiscovered. He could hear voices along the corridor; they were searching his apartments. They hadn't found anything and they sounded frustrated.

'Have you finished? We must get into a position where we can ambush the second two.'

'We've done here, my lord. We'll leave them behind the door – if anyone looks in they'll not see them.' Robin grinned. 'But they'll smell them, that's for sure.'

'Don't shoot to kill, there has been more than enough of that in the past twenty-four hours. Though given the choice, I'd rather be shot than hanged.'

He walked along the carpeted centre of the passageway, knowing the men were searching his bedchamber. He intended to position himself outside the sitting-room door. He couldn't hear what the men were saying but he was sure they hadn't found Hester. Wherever she had secreted herself, he hoped she would remain quiet until this final part of the drama was completed.

He gestured to the others to hide, and once again stood where he would be in full view when the door opened. The shock of seeing him, armed to the teeth would, he hoped, be enough to freeze them in their tracks. He knew he was a formidable sight, standing well over two yards in his stockings, his face lean and weather-beaten from his years fighting Bonaparte. He looked what he was, a battle-hardened veteran.

He gripped the butts of his guns firmly and braced himself. This time the door was flung open, no attempt at deception.

'Bugger me!'

These were the last words the leader of the gang said, as Ralph smashed him squarely on the jaw with his pistol and he fell backwards, unconscious, with a crash. The man behind him gave up without a murmur. Ralph thought he must have seen the pile of bodies in the outhouse and feared if he so much as blinked he would join them.

'Don't bother to do more than truss them, Robin, we have them all. He has no one else to warn.'

'Yes, my lord. There's still the other two downstairs to deal with. Shall we do that whilst you find Miss Frobisher?'

'Yes. They won't have heard anything, the kitchen's too far away. Here, take my pistols, I'll not need them.'

He walked along the passageway trying to think as Hester might have done – where would she have chosen to hide? He turned back, calling out to Robin. 'Ask the one that's conscious where they've searched.'

Robin did so and the man was happy to oblige with what he knew. They'd looked through all the downstairs rooms and those on the first floor, so where the hell was she? She must be in the attics. There were large rooms on the third floor, not occupied by servants, used as nurseries and schoolrooms in the distant past. She had to be up there, as there was no where else to look.

Thirty minutes later he still hadn't found her and was beginning to feel the first flicker of alarm. He shouted and called her name; if she was unharmed, she must have heard him. Why hadn't she answered?

He pounded back down the stairs coming face-to-face with Robin, looking grave. 'I have very bad news, my lord. The bastards killed one of the girls, little Meg, they broke her neck.' Robin continued, 'Miss Bird suffered a concussion when they threw her down the steps of the root cellar and is still out cold; Polly is taking care of her. Tom has carried the poor lady upstairs to her chamber and they are making her as comfortable as they can. My fear is it will be the cold that kills her, not the head injury.

'They were shut in all this time, and it's bloody freezing down there.'

Ralph rubbed his eyes. How many more people would suffer before things returned to normal? 'What about James? Did they find him?'

'No, sir, he had time to hide and they didn't bother to look too closely in there. But there's no one to send for the doctor.'

'Fred will have ridden to Squire Norton; remember, we told him if we didn't return he was to fetch help.' He knew the militia would go to Bracken Manor first, but possibly the magistrate would have the intelligence to send across to Neddingfield as well.

'Robin, I searched the nurseries and schoolrooms and she's definitely not there. She has to be somewhere on this floor; maybe she doesn't realize it's me looking for her and is too scared to come out.' He paused. 'The dog. Get downstairs and fetch him. He'll find her for us. God damn it! Why didn't I think of him sooner?'

Whilst he waited he walked back to Hester's apartments calling out her name; he listened but heard no response. Leaving the door open he went elsewhere and did the same, still no answer.

Jet galloped up the stairs greeting Ralph enthusiastically. 'Good boy, we need you to find your mistress.'

The dog sat down, his tail brushing the carpet, his liquid brown eyes fixed on his face as if waiting for instructions.

'Go, seek your mistress, find Hester.' The dog remained where he was, seemed unable to grasp the simple fact that he was needed to find the person he loved the best.

'Hell and damnation! I shall have to try again myself.' He headed back down the corridor, deciding to start with his own apartments and work his way back; she had to be somewhere. 'Hester, Hester, where are you?'

Calling her name out loud did the trick; the dog put his nose to the floor and raced ahead of him and into the sitting-room.

'Robin, with me – she must be in here. Perhaps she's unwell and unable to answer us.'

He burst into the sitting-room calling again. Again no answer. The dog had vanished, his bedchamber door was open, but she couldn't be in there, he'd looked under the bed, looked in the closets, surely he hadn't missed her? There was no cranny large enough for a full-grown woman to hide. As he reached the dressing-room Jet began to howl – the hairs on the back of his neck stood up at the mournful sound. It was the bay of an animal grieving for its owner. Please God, not now, not when it was over. How could he live without his darling girl?

The dog was sitting by the closet door, his muzzle pointed skywards, sounding like a wolf. 'Enough, Jet. Silence. Are you telling me she's in there?' He began to fling out the clothes, his jackets disregarded without a thought. 'Robin, bring a candle-stick. If the dog says she's in here, then she must be. But God knows where, the closet's empty.'

He walked in, crouching down, the candle in front of him; at first he couldn't see where she might be hiding, then he spied a narrow space running behind the shelves. God's teeth! Was she squashed in there?

'Robin, I've found her. We have to move the shelves and do it fast.'

He pushed the candle into the crevice and, at the far end, he could see a crumpled shape. 'My love, Hester, speak to me.' She remained silent and he didn't know if she was alive. Handing the candle to Robin he swung back, gripping the rear of the shelves with both hands, then threw himself backwards. They didn't move. He was about to try again when Robin tapped him on the shoulder.

'We'll not do it that way, my lord. We have to work from the front, I helped the carpenter install something similar in your rooms. I know how they fit together.'

Ralph backed out from the closet and jumped to the front of the shelves. Not bothering to remove the neat piles of undergarments and shirts, he took hold of the wood and with Robin gripping the other side heaved with all his strength. There was some movement. Two further massive pulls and the nails tore from the floor and, in a tumble of splintering wood and folded clothes, he fell over.

The dust swirled around him, but ignoring it he scrambled out from under the debris and stepped back inside the ruined closet. As the shelves had crashed forward she had toppled to the floor. Reaching down to grip her under the arms, he lifted her gently. Resting her over his shoulder he backed into the dressing-room and then out to his bedchamber.

He carried her over to the huge bed and placed her on it putting his ear to her lips; he believed there was warmth on his face, but he wasn't sure. His fingers rested under her jaw and ran back to the juncture of her neck. Yes, definitely a faint fluttering.

She was breathing, but barely. Ineffectually chafing her limp hands between his he called her name in vain.

Then the fog cleared from his brain. She had been deprived of air, if he could refill her lungs then maybe that would restore her.

'Get the shutters back and open the window; we need fresh air in here, Robin.' He looked down; was it possible for him to expedite the process? A quack had blown his own breath into the mouth of a man who'd been fished out of a lake. The result had been miraculous, perhaps this would work with Hester.

What had the doctor done exactly? He couldn't remember the precise procedure, but matters could hardly be made worse. Ralph knelt on the edge of the bed filling his lungs, covered her nose with one hand pulled her chin down with the other. Then he placed his lips over hers in order to expel his breath into her open mouth. Lifting his head he repeated the process.

A sudden blast of freezing air shook the bed hangings. Gulping in a third lungful of this fresh air he bent down to place his mouth over hers for a final time. Her mouth felt less cold, was his strange approach working?

Bending down, he scooped her up in his arms. 'I'm going to take her over to the window, it might revive her.'

Robin held on to the open shutters to prevent them banging in the gale that had developed during the morning. He looked down. To his astonishment and wonder a pair of hazel eyes stared back at him.

'My darling, thank God, thank God. I thought I'd lost you.'

'I'm more likely to die of cold, than anything else, if you persist in holding me in front of an open window, my love.' Her voice was no more than a whisper, but her tone was light showing she had suffered no damage to her mind after her near suffocation in the closet.

'Shut the window, Robin.' Reluctant to release his hold, he wanted to crush her to his chest, smother her with kisses, tell her that his life would also have ended if she had perished. Instead he placed her carefully on her feet, keeping his arm around her shoulders in case her knees were weak.

'Whatever possessed you to squeeze in behind those shelves? If I hadn't found you when I did ...'

'There's no need to say it, I know. In fact, I knew immediately that I'd made a dreadful mistake. I was terrified, knew I must hide until you came back. It was the only place I could find.'

She leant against him, resting her face on his chest. He heard Robin leave the room, giving them some privacy. 'It's cold in here, sweetheart, let's return to the kitchen; you'll soon be warm down there.'

'Ralph, tell me, is everything well downstairs? It wasn't cowardice that made me run away when I heard them coming in – I knew they'd come to murder me. I believed if I remained free the others would be safer. The men would be more concerned with finding me than harming them.'

He hesitated, should he tell her what had transpired, or wait until she was fully recovered? 'I have grave news for you, my love: poor little Meg was killed and your dearest friend, Miss Bird, was knocked out. I intend to send Robin at once to fetch the physician now everything else has been settled.'

Chapter Twenty-two

MEG KILLED? HOW could that have happened? It was all her fault, if these monsters hadn't been seeking her out the poor girl would be alive still. Birdie, her dearest friend, injured – it was too much to bear. 'I must go to her at once. My chest feels a little sore, but apart from that, and a slight headache, I'm fully recovered.'

She wriggled out of his restraint, almost running along the passageway; taking the back stairs would be a quicker option but it would mean searching for a candlestick.

'I take it you discovered who was behind the attacks?' she asked him, as she hurried down the stairs.

'The man behind it refused to give his real name, and I didn't dare wait to discover it. I knew you were in danger.'

'What did you do with him?' She prayed that he hadn't killed him, she hated to think of the people who had died over the past few days.

'I overpowered him; he's tied up, locked in a cupboard. I shall leave the magistrate to discover his identity. My main concern is to take care of you and Miss Bird.'

Hester didn't go into the kitchen, she ran straight past and up the stairs that led to the rooms she'd been sharing with Birdie. Her friend was lying quietly, eyes closed, her slight form barely making a shape under the coverlets.

'Polly, how is she? Has she shown any signs of waking?'

'Miss Bird's much warmer, Miss Frobisher, and her breathing's steady enough; I reckon the bang on her head gave her a bit of a concussion. She'll be as right as rain by tomorrow, you mark my words.'

'I'll take over here, Polly. You go to your room and change. Then go to the kitchen and find yourself something to eat and drink. Without Miss Bird to organize matters, we shall have to rely on Tom. His baking's appalling, but he can put the kettle on well enough.'

Her attempt to at humour had the desired effect and the girl's face lightened. 'Thank you, miss, I should be right glad to remove these dirty clothes, it was that filthy in the root cellar, I can tell you. Would it be in order if I borrowed…?' The girl's eyes filled.

'Yes, of course. Meg has no need of her belongings now. Lord Colebrook will make sure her parents are recompensed for their daughter's sad demise. I'm sure they'll not need her garments returned immediately.'

Polly curtsied, leaving her alone with the person she loved most in the world, apart from her darling Ralph. The room was warm, the fire huge and the curtains closed. She straightened the covers, checking for herself that Birdie was breathing, then pulled across a small padded armchair to the bed.

It was strange to sit in a room with the curtains drawn when it was scarcely noon. She walked briskly to the windows, flinging back the heavy material and pulling open the shutters with a bang. She refused to sit in darkness as if her friend was already in Heaven. The fire was sufficient, and the small window, halfway up the outer wall, did not let in draughts.

She could see only the kitchen gardens and beyond to the woods from her vantage point. It was a depressing view when the skies were heavy with unshed rain, and the sun hidden firmly behind the clouds. She returned to her vigil, praying for her friend, hoping that somehow good could come out of the evil that had been done that day.

Ralph returned to collect his boots only to discover they had vanished. Where the hell were they? He wasn't in the mood for practical jokes. He twitched the curtains away to check a second time, but they were still gone. He straightened, frowning out of the window.

Good God! His eyes widened as he stared across the park to the long gravelled drive. Like a circus parade, headed by the scarlet uniforms of a company of militia, followed a large coach and two small closed carriages, whilst bringing up the rear some half a mile distant was a small body of townsfolk, parcels and bags under their arms. The missing servants were returning.

His laughter rang around the room. Who the occupants of the carriages might be he had no inkling, but unless he found his boots he would have to greet them, and the commander of the militia, in his stockings.

Hester heard a commotion outside the door and Polly burst in, her face smiling and her ruined gown replaced by a clean blue dress and pristine apron and cap.

'Miss Frobisher, Tom was about to go to town when his lordship appeared looking for his boots and saying that the militia are coming, plus three carriages and the staff that left last week.'

Hester smiled. She'd quite forgotten the notes she'd sent with the lawyers in all the excitement. 'Lord Colebrook has lost his boots? Do you know, I haven't noticed he was without them when he was here earlier.'

Polly giggled. 'They weren't lost really, miss, his man had taken them downstairs to give them a clean. They have been restored to him now. I've brought you some coffee and what is left of the plum cake. His lordship insisted that you have something to eat and drink.'

'Thank you; I'm not hungry, but the coffee is exactly what I need. Go back, Polly, tell Seth and Robert to start lighting fires in the main part of the house and the apartments. We shall transfer there later today.' She smiled fondly at her friend so worryingly still in the bed. 'And as soon as Miss Bird's recovered she shall move into the chambers next to mine. Her days of acting as housekeeper and cook are done with. She's all I have in the world, and I shall not let her work for her living ever again.'

'Miss Bird's a lady and should not be obliged to live in the servants' quarters, as if she was something else.'

'Quite right, Polly. From now on she is one of the family.'

Hester drank the coffee, the bitter taste reviving her wonderfully. She hoped the doctor would be in one of the carriages Polly had mentioned, but she feared that the other would contain the vicar. Whatever would the reverend gentleman make of the chaos that was Neddingfield at the moment?

Twenty minutes later there was a soft tap at the door and an unfamiliar maidservant came in and curtsied. 'Begging your pardon, Miss Frobisher, but I have the doctor here to see Miss Bird.'

'Excellent, please show him in; I have been expecting him.'

Doctor Radcliff smiled at her. 'Good morning, Miss Frobisher. I have come to examine your patient. This is a nasty business all round, but at least I can see that you are now fully recovered from your accident two weeks ago.'

She looked at him blankly. Was it so little time since all this started? It seemed like a lifetime, so much had happened. 'Miss Bird has a steady pulse, but I'm so worried she hasn't regained consciousness.' She went to wait by the window, leaving the physician to do his job. After a remarkably brief time the man straightened and turned to her, a broad smile on his face.

'Has Miss Bird been overtaxing herself lately?' Puzzled, she nodded. 'In that case it explains what's going on. She's deeply asleep whilst her body mends itself. She must have been exhausted by whatever has been going on here, and the bang on the head has merely pushed her body into a deep restorative slumber.'

'She's not concussed?'

'No, Miss Frobisher, your companion's asleep. I advise you leave her to her slumbers whilst I go and examine the second patient, the young man with a bullet through his shoulder.'

'Thank you, I shall go down with the good news.' Outside the new maid was waiting anxiously.

'Excuse me, miss, I'm to conduct the doctor to James now.'

Hester nodded. She caught a glimpse of her dishevelled appearance in the over-mantel mirror and paused, horrified. Her hair was in disarray, half up, half down, her face besmirched, and what had been a dismal gown was now a total disaster. She could not possibly meet the vicar looking as she did, but all her belongings were hanging in the cupboard where Birdie slept. She couldn't go back in there and disturb her friend.

She heard another set of footsteps on the stairs and looked round to see her own abigail, Jane. 'Good heavens! What are you doing here?'

The girl curtsied. 'We were held up by the snow, miss, but as soon as it cleared Bill set off and here we are. Not a moment too soon neither. I've had your trunks taken to your rooms. There will be something amongst them that is not too creased so you can change before going downstairs.'

She smiled. 'I'm sure whatever you find will be better than what I have on at present.'

Ralph was in the drawing-room, the fire doing little to dispel the damp and cold that had accumulated whilst the room had been disused. His boots restored, his jacket brushed, and the worst of the mud sponged from his britches, he looked every inch the lord of the manor.

He had been shocked, but delighted, to discover the occupant of the second carriage was Mr Blunt, the vicar of Little Neddingfield. Hester had been busy in his absence – he still had no idea how she had sent the notes, and could hardly ask the gentleman perched nervously on the edge of his seat. No, he would have to contain his impatience until she arrived. The larger carriage, he should have recognized, belonged Hester.

He'd left Robin and Tom to deal with the young lieutenant, as he had no further interest in the matter. His mind was firmly fixed on marrying his beloved as speedily as possible.

He turned and his heart caught in his throat. Standing in the doorway was a young woman he scarcely recognized. Her hair was piled in a glorious russet coronet, her green eyes huge in her oval face, and she was wearing a ravishing, high-waisted gown in gold and green, that exactly matched her eyes. She looked enchanting and she was all his.

'Lord Colebrook, Mr Blunt, I sincerely apologize for keeping you waiting. It's so kind of you to come with such alacrity. No doubt his lordship has explained the urgency?'

Ralph blinked. Good God! Surely she was not alluding to their pre-empting the marriage service? If not, then he was as much in the dark as Blunt.

Blunt bowed deeply, obviously impressed. 'No, Miss Frobisher, we have waited for you before discussing anything.'

'Please be seated, both of you. Shall I begin?'

Ralph listened with incredulity as she explained, mainly for his benefit, that their Aunt Agatha had moved to live on the Continent and left her English estates jointly to them. Hester explained that until they were united as man and wife the estates would languish untended, as neither of them would be in the position to move matters forward. He hid his smile, she was talking total fustian, but Blunt seemed convinced.

'Of course, my lord, Miss Frobisher. If you would kindly supply me with the necessary details, I shall expedite matters at once. As you have both been in residence here already for two weeks, there's no difficulty on that score. Will the first week in December be suitable?'

'Perfectly, Blunt. My man and Miss Frobisher's can supply you with the information you need.' He stood and bowed formally; the man took his cue, scrambling to his feet.

'Good morning, my lord, madam, I shall look forward to conducting your wedding ceremony in three weeks' time.'

A parlourmaid curtsied and ushered the vicar out. Ralph followed him, closing the door before holding out his arms.

'Ralph, we must not. There are still things we don't know, loose ends to tie.'

Reluctantly he nodded; she was right, until the militia removed the prisoner from the secret passage, the corpses from the outbuildings, and he had discovered the identity of the man behind the attacks, they could not relax.

'I suppose you wish me to ride with the militia when they go?'

'I do, my love. There are so many things I don't understand. How did this man know so much about Neddingfield and Aunt Agatha's affairs?'

'Can't it wait until tomorrow? I can think of far better things to do....'

'Enough, my lord. What happened last night will not take place again until we are wed.'

He grinned and kissed her gently. 'We shall discuss that later, when I return.'

He could hear her laughing as he strode off to find the officer leading the troops. Robin told him the young man was waiting in the study eager to impart some news.

Ralph nodded to the officer. 'My lord, Captain Carstairs found the perpetrator of this nasty business gibbering in a broom cupboard. The man's name is Bertram Sinclair, his father, also Bertram, was a remote connection, a cousin of your aunt's. It appears he gained his knowledge of Neddingfield Hall from his father whose grandfather lived here years ago. By your demise he believed he stood next in line.'

'Go on, man, tell me the rest. Did Captain Carstairs find out how Sinclair thought he could murder us and still claim the title?'

'It would seem, my lord, he believed creating an atmosphere of fear around this place meant nobody would come to investigate your disappearance, or that of Miss Frobisher. Then, after a time, he was going to reappear and claim the title and your fortunes.'

Ralph shook his head. 'The plans of a madman! He couldn't claim the title without producing my body and by doing so, would incriminate himself. His scheme was ingenious but fatally flawed.' He nodded, dismissing the soldier. 'Thank you for your assistance. I shall detain you no longer.' He strode back to the drawing-room but his quarry had gone. He met Polly who smiled and pointed upstairs. Even better – it would be easier to convince his darling girl that they were as good as married if she was already in her bedchamber.